MANANNÁN'S PEARL

MERROWKIN BOOK 3

JENNIFER ALLIS PROVOST

CONTENTS

THE MERROWS ARE COMING

"**M**eri," my mother called as the bedroom door banged open. "Meri! Are you awake?"

I blinked my eyes open. "I am now."

"Get ready," she said. "The merrows will be arriving soon!"

I sat up and looked at the window. It was pitch black outside. "They're arriving before sunrise? But the ceremony won't be until four."

"Yes, well, down below they do things their own way," Mama said. "Where's Aodhan?"

"Here, Mrs Murphy," Aodhan said, as he raised an arm to reveal his location. He was clear across the room, curled up in the armchair and nestled under a blanket. I'd been shuttled to his room the day prior so Aunt Donna and her wife could use mine while they stayed with us for my parents' vow renewal weekend. Since my room used to be Donna's, it was only fair. Besides, I liked being in Aodhan's room.

"How can I help?" Aodhan asked. "Just point me toward what needs doing."

"Aodhan you are a treasure," Mama said. "I'm not really sure what we need to do first. Make some coffee for the guests, maybe? Or tea?"

"I can handle both," I said, as I stretched the last bits of sleep from my muscles. "We also finished all the baking yesterday, so we'll be able to put together a nice breakfast for whomever shows up in these predawn hours. Why don't you let us worry about all of that, and find someplace quiet so you can relax for a bit?"

Mama crossed the room and kissed the top of my head. "Meri girl, I don't know what I would do without you. Thank you, my lamb."

With that, Mama swept out of Aodhan's room, and proceeded to barge into Kevin's across the hall. While she harangued my brother and Kelsey, Aodhan left his uncomfortable looking chair and slid under the blankets with me. "Good morning, beautiful."

"Good morning." He gathered me against him and tucked my head underneath his chin, and all was right with my world. "When did you go to the chair?" I asked, since we'd fallen asleep together in the bed last night.

"After you went to sleep," he said. "I didn't want to violate any versions of your dad's 'no air mattress' rule."

I giggled, because I remembered that rule all too well. Aodhan and I had just gotten in some trouble at the Cliffs of Moher Visitor Centre, and Da came to rescue us. After he heard Aodhan's mother go on about how she found us sleeping on an air mattress, Da had banned them from the house as a euphemism for Aodhan and me not getting in bed together. "That was a stressful day."

"It certainly was, and it's all the more reason to make sure things go smoothly today." Aodhan caressed my cheek, then he kissed me. "Let's go have a vow renewal, shall we?"

"Let's."

I snuck into my room to get ready, and managed to change into a tee shirt and shorts without waking either of my aunts. That done, I went to the kitchen and found Da already hard at work.

"You should not be up this early," I admonished. "At this rate, you'll be dead asleep when you should be exchanging vows."

"Don't you worry about me, Meri girl," Da said, as he whisked a few pastry shells out of the oven. "I'm far too excited to sleep. Get me the pastry crème from the fridge, please?"

I did as asked. "What are you making? I thought all the baking was done."

"These are a few special tarts, for Aoife's ma," he replied, as he rinsed off some berries.

"You make special tarts for a goddess?" While I didn't know what Niamh specifically ruled over, she was the daughter of the sea god, Manannán man Lir, who also happened to be the king of the Otherworld. She must be the goddess of something.

"That I do, and how it all came about is a fine story," he replied. "One day, shortly before Kevin came along, I was trying out new dessert recipes. Your ma had gone into the town for something, and, as you know, it's nice to cook in a quiet house."

"It is," I agreed. "Can I help with these tarts?"

"Melt the apple jelly for me, so I can use it as a glaze, if you wouldn't mind," he said, as he filled a piping bag with the crème.

I found the jar of jelly quickly enough, then I scooped some into a pan and set it on the hob. "You said you were trying out new desserts?"

"Ah, yes. I was. I had just pulled a batch out of the oven when there was a knock at the door. I opened it, and standing there on the stoop was a woman with long golden hair who claimed to be a friend of Aoife's. I invited her in, made her some tea, and fed her a few berry tarts. And that's how I met Niamh."

"You won her over with a tart," I said, remembering how Niamh had warmly greeted Da when they'd seen each other following Donn Dumhach's defeat in front of the surf shop.

"That I did, and we've gotten on well ever since," Da said. "Speaking of which, best heat up that clam stew you made for the old goat. He doesn't have a sweet tooth like his bride."

"Do you get along at all with Grandfather?" I asked, as I hauled the stew pot out of the fridge and set it on the stove.

"Yes and no," Da replied. "Steinar loves his children very much, and more than anything, he wants them to be happy. Aoife is happy with me, therefore he is happy with me. However," he paused to take the apple jelly off the heat, and pour it through a fine sieve, "we met under rather awkward circumstances."

"Was it when you hit Corentin? The prince from Ker Ys she was supposed to marry?" I asked, eager for undersea gossip.

"That boy got hit because he wouldn't take no for an answer," Da said. "Your ma was wearing this dress that didn't cover one of her shoulders, and he put his hand on her bare skin. She knocked his hand away and told him to stop. He did it again, so I took it upon myself to persuade him to leave Aoife be."

"The way I heard it, you left the prince lying in a puddle of blood," came a voice from the doorway. I turned around, and saw a woman who was a taller and more heavily muscled version of my mother leaning against the doorframe. She was wearing a bronze coloured sleeveless shirt and matching pants, brown boots, and a set of gold bracelets that matched my mother's pair. She also had a long blonde plait, and striking blue eyes.

"Corentin claims you disfigured him for life," she continued.

"That will teach him to touch a woman without first securing her permission," Da said. "Meri, meet your Aunt Scáthach."

"You're The Shadow?" I blurted out.

"That old nickname," Scáthach said, with a smile. "Hello, Meri. Brian, what have you made for me?"

"I roasted a joint of mutton in the fire out back. You can go at it with your teeth." Da wiped his hands on a tea towel, then he and Scáthach embraced. "Good to see you."

"And you," she said. "Is that clam stew I smell?"

"Meri made it," Da said. Scáthach sidled over to the stove, and had a sniff.

"May I try it?" she asked.

"Of course." I got a clean spoon and handed it over. "It's still a bit cool, but you'll get the idea."

She sampled a spoonful, and grinned. "Oh, you'll be the old goat's favorite after he has this."

"Why does everyone call Grandfather a goat?" I asked, then I heard the thunder of Aodhan galloping down the stairs. He bounded into the kitchen, and stopped short when he saw Scáthach standing over the stove.

"Um, hello," Aodhan said. "I was just going to go out back, and start setting up chairs."

"I'll help," Scáthach said, then she strode out of the kitchen door and into the garden.

"Two questions," Aodhan began. "Who is that, and is there breakfast?"

"She's my Aunt Scáthach, and I will make you breakfast." I set a skillet on the stove. "How hungry are you? Ravenous as usual?"

"You know me well." Aodhan smiled at me, nodded toward my da, then he followed my aunt into the garden.

"I wonder who else will turn up before dawn." I grabbed a bowl, and started cracking eggs into it. "At this rate we'll run out of food by noon."

"If we've enough food to keep Aodhan fed, we've enough for everyone," Da said. The pastry shells had cooled, and he was piping in a layer of crème. "My true worry is the cake my mother is bringing."

I stopped moving, my whisk motionless in the eggs. "Granny Mer made a cake?"

"Claims she outdid herself," Da said. "Said it'll put her Easter cakes to shame."

"Oh, dear."

GUESTS AND GIFTS

M ama was correct, and the merrows began arriving in twos and threes just after sunrise. After we'd finished up setting out tables and chairs, and offered coffee and tea to our guests, I left Aodhan and Kevin in charge and went to get ready with Kelsey.

This past month had been a new experience for me and my brother, since he now had a live-in girlfriend, and I ended up with the closest thing to a sister I'd ever had. Despite the years of bad blood between us, this newer, happier version of Kelsey and I got on splendidly. I'd been wary at first, but after Kelsey had got into a relationship with Kevin, she hadn't reverted to her old mean girl persona even once. It made me wonder if her former best friend, Sarah, really was the mastermind behind all of their mad schemes. Kelsey maintained that Sarah was the true bully, and I was inclined to believe her.

For the ceremony, Kelsey and I were serving as maids of honor. Kelsey had chosen to wear a light blue dress, which perfectly matched her eyes. My own dress was burgundy, and it had a high halter neckline and a side slit that bordered on scandalous. Since the dress left my shoulders exposed, the scars I'd gotten from when Paul Flynn—a gancanagh who had been masquerading as the headmaster's son—attacked me were on full display.

We hadn't seen hide nor hair of Paul since Kelsey set his house on fire with him in it. And that headmaster? He was actually an ankou, also known as a soul eater. I'd routed his sorry arse, and he hadn't been seen since. Good riddance to both.

"Want me to put some concealer on those?" Kelsey asked, as she nodded toward the four round marks that were caused by the gancanagh's fingers burning into me.

"I don't mind them being seen," I said. "After all, I survived Paul's mad plans. You did, too."

"Only because of you." She leaned closer to the mirror and applied some mascara to her ginger lashes. "I have to say, even though I was trapped in his house for two days, it was worth it."

"What?" I demanded. "How could losing your free will to that monster ever be worth it?"

"Look at my life now," she said. "I have Kevin, and my friendship with you, and a million other good things. I can't imagine living without Kevin. If the price of a better life was spending a few days with that monster, so be it."

"When you put it that way, I suppose I agree." My life had also improved, since the incident involving Kelsey and me being trapped in the gancanagh's house had made Aodhan and me closer than ever. "What's next for you and Kevin? Babies?"

"Not on your life." Kelsey extended her right arm, and pointed to a small raised line on her biceps. "I've got that birth control implant. It works for three years."

"Really." I grazed my fingertip across the thin ridge under her skin. I'd wondered how those two would handle becoming parents, and based on all the time they spent holed up in Kevin's room, it seemed rather inevitable. But it seemed that they'd already thought about that. "What's it like?"

"It's not bad. They numb you, then it's just a little pinch when it goes in."

"Not the implant," I clarified. "Being with someone. Generally speaking," I added, since the last thing I wanted to hear were details about my brother.

"Well, since I've only been with Kevin, I only have him to go by," she began.

"Really?" I asked, surprised. "Sarah made it seem like you had a new boyfriend every week."

"What can I say? Sarah's a jerk to everyone. Why did I hang out with her for so long?"

"We all did foolish things when we were younger," I said. "Sorry I believed that stuff about you."

Kelsey smiled. "It's okay. As for being with someone, it's amazing. You feel loved and safe, and the absolute centre of his world." She eyed me. "Can I ask you something?"

"Ask away."

"How is it that you and Aodhan always end up in the same room, yet you don't sleep together?"

"We sleep together all the time," I said. "We just never take our clothes off."

"Aodhan doesn't ask for more?" she pressed. "Like, ever?"

"No. He never has." I thought about all the times I'd settled into his arms, and he kissed my forehead before we went to sleep. "I think he might be following my lead."

"Hm." Kelsey swiped on some lip gloss. "Maybe tonight you can remove a sock. Give the guy a few ideas, unless he's waiting for marriage."

I set down my brush and gaped at her. "Do you think he is?"

Kelsey shrugged. "No idea, but it's the only reason I can think of. Unless you've told him you don't want to?"

"I've never told him anything, not that he's ever asked," I said. "But he does always pull back when things get a bit heated." I glanced at her. "But Kevin never did?"

"He was more nervous than I was," Kelsey said. "We were both nervous, hands shaking and the like, but more than anything we wanted to be together." She faced me, and continued, "Here's the thing. Aodhan is so obviously in love with you, and you love him, too. If you want to know why he pulls back, ask him."

I swallowed hard. "What if I don't like his answer?"

"If you don't like it, you'll have to deal with it," she said. "But won't it be better to know the truth?"

"Yes," I said. "I suppose it will."

After we finished getting dressed and made up, Kelsey and I rejoined the rest in the garden. More merrows had arrived, including my grandfather, King Steinar the Immoveable, ruler of Kilstiffen. I found him standing with Kevin and Da near the buffet table.

"Grandfather," I said as I embraced him. "I made clam stew for you."

"Thank you, Meri," he said as he patted my back. "You remain my favorite granddaughter."

"She's our only granddaughter," my grandmother, Niamh, said as she approached us. I went right from Grandfather's arms to hers. "How are you, my dear?"

"I'm well," I said. "How was your journey above?"

"Swift," she replied, which I inferred as good. Behind Niamh, I saw a gathering of people who appeared to be from below, but who were standing apart from those from Kilstiffen.

"Who are those people?" I asked.

"They are delegates from other sea kingdoms," Grandfather replied. "The marriage of one of Kilstiffen's daughters is a momentous occasion. They've come bearing gifts from their respective lands."

"Are all the sea kingdoms represented?" I asked. "Even Ker Ys?"

"Ker Ys sent a delegate, and it is not Nahel," Grandfather replied. "I may have told Gradlon that his children are not to come within fifty paces of you or Kevin ever again."

"That's fantastic," I said. "And that's why you're my favorite king."

Grandfather gave me a sly look as Niamh burst into laughter. "I see which side of your lineage you favor," Grandfather said.

"I'd say she's a perfect blend of the two," Niamh said, as she smoothed my hair. "Speaking of which, I believe you have more guests arriving."

Niamh was right, and our guests of the human variety wandered into the garden in groups of twos and threes. Despite all my worries, they got on well with the merrows and others from below. Even Aodhan's mother, who tended to be suspicious of everyone she didn't already know, and a fair few of those she was acquainted with, laughed at a few of the merrows' stories. Then again, she had been married to Donn Dumhach, the sidhe prince of the dead. After living with him for seven years, talking with a merrow probably didn't faze her in the least.

The ceremony itself was a thing of beauty. Da wore the same dark suit he'd worn when he first married Mama all those years ago, and it still fit him perfectly. As for my mother, she wore a white knee length dress overlaid with intricate lace, and carried orange and pink roses in her bouquet with a matching flower crown on her head. And when my parents took their place at the top of the aisle and looked at each another, no one doubted how much they still loved each other.

The officiant for the ceremony was none other than Sister Mary Katherine. Since school was still closed down indefinitely, she had plenty of free time, and had readily agreed to perform the ceremony. Perhaps she would embark on a new career, and leave teaching behind altogether.

As my parents said their vows, the various merrows in attendance began to sing. Their song was soft at first, but it soon grew in volume and emotion as it resonated around my parents, honoring them and their renewed commitment to one another. For once, I had no desire to join the chorus and was content to listen. While they sang, Aodhan slipped his arm around my waist and kissed the soft spot behind my ear.

"Beautiful," he murmured. "So incredibly beautiful."

We served Granny Mer's cake after the ceremony. It was a hulking five layered beast of chocolate sponge and filled with her homemade cherry jam, and it was slathered with the richest chocolate buttercream frosting ever whipped up. That cake was the most delicious thing I had ever eaten.

While most of the guests ate, the representatives from the sea kingdoms approached my parents and bestowed various offerings to them; honestly, the whole thing was a bit creepy, like an old folk horror movie. When it became the council of lords' turn to present their offerings, they also brought out gifts for myself and Kevin, which turned out to be a matching set of bracelets.

"These bracelets represent the seas," the councilor said. They were as wide as the golden cuffs my mother and Scáthach wore, and were studded with blue gems. "All we are comes from the sea, and to the sea we will someday return."

"Thank you," I said, though I had half a mind to toss the bracelets in their faces. Did they think we'd forgotten their mad scheme to make Grandfather abdicate his throne, or how they turned half of Kilstiffen against my mother? But to bring up their bad behavior would cause an uproar on my parents' special day, and that just wouldn't do.

"We appreciate these very much," I said eventually.

After the council members departed, Kevin whispered, "Think Kelsey will like this?"

I gazed at the gaudy bracelet in his hand. My brother had never worn a piece of jewelry in his life, and I couldn't imagine him ever putting this ornate mass of gold on his wrist. "Probably, if for no other reason than it's from you," I said.

Just when it seemed like all the gifts had been handed out, an excited murmur rolled over the crowd. Everyone turned toward the bottom of the garden, then Manannán mac Lir himself strode into view. The guests parted like the sea, and Manannán stopped directly in front of my parents.

"Congratulations on your second wedding day," Manannán said. "I daresay this day is even more special than the first."

"Aye, Grandfather," Mama said, as she looped her arm with Da's, and smiled at me and Kevin. "The first time was perfect, but now that our children are here to witness us renewing our vows, my heart can hardly contain itself."

"Yes, sir," Da said. "Thank you, for blessing us with your presence."

"You don't just get my presence," Manannán said. "I've brought gifts, as well." From the folds of his cloak, he produced a cauldron and a sword.

"Brian, it's plain how you adore Aoife, but you do love feeding people almost as much as you love my granddaughter," he began. "This cauldron will make sure you always have enough food, no matter how many portions you dole out."

"Thank you, Manannán," Da said, as he accepted the cauldron. "Truly, thank you."

"And for you, my warrior child," Manannán continued, "I've had this sword knocking about for some time, and I believe you will put it to good use. It's called Fragarach."

"It's beautiful," Mama said, as Manannán handed it to her hilt first. "You're certain you're willing to part with it?"

"I can think of no one better suited to wield it than you, the champion of Kilstiffen," Manannán replied.

Mama grinned, then she completed a few flourishes with the sword. "Thank you, Grandfather. I can't wait to stab something in your honor."

A GARDEN PARTY?

Later on, after the excitement of being visited by our godliest relation had wound down, the party quieted to a dull roar. The guests milled about, drinking and visiting with each other, and nibbling cakes. Everyone was happy and well fed, which was just as it should be.

Aodhan stood behind me and wrapped his arm around my shoulders. "We should have one of these."

"What? A garden party?"

"No. A wedding."

I moved so my cheek was resting against Aodhan's chest, and saw my brother and Kelsey standing near the greenhouse. Their heads were close together, and they were smiling at each other. "I suppose Kevin and Kelsey will be next."

"Not for them." Aodhan put his mouth close to my ear. "For us."

Was he joking? He had to be. "We can't get married. We're too young."

"You will be eighteen in two days."

"That's still awfully young."

"How long will you make me wait, then? Six months?"

"We will still be eighteen in six months! Maybe in a few years. Like, five."

"One."

"Four."

"Two."

"Three."

"Fine." He kissed the side of my head. "In three years, you'll marry me. Unless I can sway you to my cause, and we make it official earlier."

"Stop teasing me," I said. "I know why you're so eager. You want to have sex."

Lips pressed against my ear, he murmured, "Believe it or not, marriage is not required for that."

"Then why do you always stop before we get to it?" I demanded, loudly enough for a few heads to turn in our direction. Aodhan opened his mouth, then he glanced around the yard and turned my body to face him.

"Can those from below read lips? Because we have an audience." With his eyes, he indicated a few interested parties, the nosy council of lords included. I had no idea if any of them could read lips, or if they had super sharp hearing, but I did know that Aodhan and I were not done with this conversation.

"Meet me in my room in ten minutes," I said, then I remembered that my aunts were staying my room, and therefore we would have little to no privacy there. "Actually, let's meet in your room."

Eyes wide, he nodded. "Ten it is, Mer."

Aodhan kissed my forehead, then we went off in separate directions. I watched as he chased after his younger sisters, and smiled as he caught Roan and turned her upside down in his arms. He was so good with people, and especially with children, and I was lucky to have him in my life.

But we couldn't get married. That was ridiculous.

I crossed the garden, and found my mother and her sister admitting the sword Manannán had given to Mama. "Have you killed anyone with that yet?" I asked.

"No, but the day is young." Mama looped me in for a hug, and crushed a few of the roses in her hair in the process. "Meri, Scáthach was wondering when you'd like to visit her in Evonium."

"Isn't that a military academy?" I asked. While I like visiting new places, I wasn't overly fond of combat, especially combat that involved me.

"Evonium is its own kingdom, much like Kilstiffen," Scáthach replied. "The academy is a small part of what we do."

"Aodhan would certainly appreciate having a look at the training fields," Mama said.

"I'm sure he would," I said. "Aodhan loves anything he can turn into a sport." As if on cue, Aodhan swiveled around and met my gaze, then he grinned and waved at us. "He's also got ears like a bat."

Mama and Scáthach shared a look. "It's not his ears, but his heart that hears you," my aunt said.

"Aodhan's heart can hear things?" I asked.

"No, silly," Scáthach said. "A merrow's mate can hear their song, even when the merrow in question is silent."

I watched as Aodhan romped with his sisters, and remembered all the times he heard what I was muttering, even though I was certain I hadn't been speaking out loud. "But Aodhan's not a merrow."

"He doesn't have to be," Mama said. "Your father is no merrow, but he heard me lamenting my defeat as clear as a bell, and followed my voice all the way to the Cliffs, where he found me on that beach."

"It was the same with our parents," Scáthach said. "Papa was out hunting for clams, and Mama heard him all the way in her garden. She was prepared to scour the island until she found him, and she did. They've been smitten with each other ever since." I glanced toward my grandparents, the sea king and the bright goddess. Theirs was a union that began a long, long time ago, and was still as strong as ever.

"That's... that's a lovely story," I said. "Is that why Da used to go out on his boat so much?"

"Isn't Brian a fisherman?" Scáthach countered. "Seems like he belongs on that boat."

"While Mama was gone, he went out every day and caught hardly any fish," I explained. "Was he listening for you?"

"Perhaps he was," Mama replied. "But I was too far below for him to hear me. The magic is strong, but not invincible."

"So if I go below, Aodhan won't hear me any longer?" I pressed.

"Why don't you want him to hear you?" Scáthach asked. "If he hears you, it's because your heart's reaching out to him."

"I don't know about that," I said in a rush. My mind was whirling with too much information, and I desperately tried to steer the conversation away from fate and magic and people hearing their true love's song. "When should we plan to visit Evonium? It's not like we have to work around our school schedule," I added. "Did you know there's talk of Sister Mary Katherine becoming headmistress?"

Mama and Scáthach shared another look; apparently my desperate attempt to change the subject had been a bit ham fisted. "Let me speak to Brian, and Kevin," Mama said. "We can plan a family holiday. Aodhan and Kelsey can come along, too."

"A holiday for us all," I said, as I watched Aodhan walk to the refreshment table and get his sisters fresh cups of juice. "How lovely."

Half an hour later than expected, I slipped into Aodhan's room and eased the door closed. He was already inside, pacing the length of the room like a caged tiger.

"I'm sorry it took me longer than ten minutes," I began, then Aodhan swept me into his arms and kissed me like he hadn't seen me in years. I was momentarily shocked, then he slid his hands down to my thighs and lifted me against him, pressing my body between his and the door. I wound my arms around his neck, and let him devour me.

When we parted, he said, "I don't want to marry you to have sex with you. I want to marry you because I love you. And I know we're young," he continued, when I began protesting, "but we've known each other for fifteen years."

"Longer than that," I said. "Mama told me she used to bring me and Kevin 'round to your place to play with you and your older sisters."

"See that? It's fate." Aodhan caressed my cheek. "You were made for me, Mer, and I was made for you. When the rest of the merrows were singing while your parents exchanged vows, and I heard you—"

"You heard me?" I asked, since I was certain I hadn't made a sound during the ceremony. I remembered what Mama and Scáthach said about a merrow's true mate being able to hear them with their heart. I felt incredulous and shocked and, more than anything, hopeful. "Heard me how?"

"Remember how I had my arm around you?" he asked. I nodded. "When the singing started, I could feel the vibration in you here." He placed his hand just below my ribcage. "It was like the song was born there, deep inside you, and spread throughout your body, and, since I was holding you, it spread through me as well."

I set one of my hands on top of his where it lay on my belly, and placed the other on his cheek. "And that's when you fell in love with me?"

"No, Mer. I fell in love with you a long time ago."

At that, my heart grew so full it shattered, only to reform bigger and stronger and absolutely spilling over with love. I opened my mouth to tell Aodhan, well, everything, but before I could get a word out, he clamped his hand over my lips.

"Hush," he said. "There are dozens of merrows right outside my window, and if they hear you singing like that, they'll all think we're, well, you know."

I hadn't realized I was singing, and I wondered if it was that special song that only Aodhan could hear. I pulled his hand away from my face. "I thought you and Kevin soundproofed all the bedrooms."

"We only did his and your parents' rooms," he said. "I couldn't do our rooms without your dad knowing, and there was a very real possibility of him murdering me if I brought it up."

"Nonsense." I wound my arms around Aodhan's neck and sank my fingers into his soft, thick hair. "Da adores you. But you have a point. We should get back out there."

"Yes, my love." Aodhan let me slide out of his arms, but he kept hold of my hand. "I am eager to continue this talk in a more private location."

I opened the door, then I glanced at him over my shoulder. "So am I."

After the sun had set, and most of the merrows had gone as stealthily as they arrived, someone took it upon themselves to light a fire in the old stone circle near the apple orchard; according to Da, times past the fire pit was used to boil water for a quick cup of tea while working outdoors. Now it was used for ambiance, and roasting the occasional sausage under the stars. We gathered around it in twos and threes as the flames reached toward the sky.

"I'd say today was nearly perfect," Aodhan murmured. He was sitting with his back against a tree stump on the edge of the orchard, and I was nestled on his lap with my cheek resting against his chest.

"It certainly was." The night was cool, but I was warm and safe in Aodhan's arms. "Da and Mama are so happy together."

"They deserve all the happiness in the world," he said, and he was right. My parents had spent fourteen long years apart, but it hadn't dampened their love in the slightest. "Want to go out on the boat tomorrow?"

"Luring me out on the water so no one can hear me scream?" I teased.

"More like so no one can hear you sing," he retorted. "Seriously, it will be as private a place to talk as any. What do you say?"

"Okay." I did want to continue our talk, and I did not want an audience any more than Aodhan did. "That sounds nice."

"I got you something. I can give it to you tomorrow."

"Do I get a hint as to what it is?"

"I ordered a wetsuit in your size, and it came in yesterday," he replied. "We need to get on your swimming lessons, what with summer coming up."

"Thank you." I honestly had no desire to swim, but it would be smart to learn, what with me being half merrow and all. "You really like the water, don't you?"

"Always have." He tightened his arms around me. "For as long as I can remember, I've been drawn to the water. Maybe that's why I've always been drawn to you."

"And here I thought you loved me."

Aodhan kissed my hair. "You know I do."

I set my hand over his heart. "I have to tell you something."

He tilted up my chin. "You can tell me anything, any time."

"I love you, too."

OUT ON THE BOAT

Getting dressed the next morning was rather difficult.

Aunts Donna and Elaine remained in my room, which was fine, but now the door was locked. I suppose the romance had affected us all last night. While I didn't begrudge them their time together, almost all of my clean clothes were in my closet.

After several minutes of knocking didn't rouse them, I decided to seek alternative wardrobe solutions. I checked the hot press and found my favorite denim shorts clean and ready to wear, so that was a win. My runners were in Aodhan's room, so all of my clothing below my waist was sorted. As for the rest, I'd have to get creative.

When I couldn't rouse Kelsey or Kevin, and therefore couldn't borrow one of Kelsey's shirts, I appealed to Aodhan.

"Of course you can wear one of my shirts," Aodhan said, and he rooted through his clothes for me. "We're only going out on the boat, anyway."

"True. It's not like it's a fashion show." He handed me one of his tee shirts, then I turned my back so I could take off the shirt I'd slept in and pull the fresh one over my head. Clothing now fresh as a daisy, I tossed the worn shirt into the laundry basket. "Have you seen my sweatshirt?"

"You mean *my* sweatshirt?" Aodhan countered, as he handed me the garment. I'd borrowed it from him on the day the gancanagh had injured my shoulder. Thanks to the attack, the sweatshirt ended up with four holes that matched my four scars. While I'd been in Kilstiffen with the healers, Talia, my mother's former attendant, had mended the sweatshirt by embroidering the holes closed with golden thread. It wasn't very practical, but the line of tiny gold shells was beautiful.

"I've claimed it, so now it's mine." I grabbed my phone. "Breakfast, then boat?"

"Perfect, beautiful."

Since no one had yet left their rooms save for myself and Aodhan, breakfast was a simple affair for just the two of us. After we'd eaten, and left a note on the kitchen table letting everyone know we were headed to the shop and were then going out on the water, we were off.

But first, we checked on the fire pit out back.

"I'm glad someone thought to put it out," I said. The ashes were soaking wet and ice cold, just as they should be. "Probably Kevin. He's the responsible one around here."

"Probably." Aodhan stood behind me and slid his arms around my waist, then he held my wrist in front of us. "You really want to wear this on the boat?" he asked, as his thumb stroked the blue stones set in the bracelet the council had given me.

"It's been growing on me." I moved my wrist back and forth, enjoying how the gems caught the light. "I'm wearing the pearl, too," I added, indicating my necklace.

"I suppose, as a princess of Kilstiffen, jewelry is your right."

"I am not a princess," I said, as I rounded on him. "If anything, I'm the heiress."

"I stand corrected," he said, with a shallow bow. "Would the heiress like to remove herself to the boat?"

My eyes narrowed even as I struggled to keep from laughing. "That sounds lovely."

And it was a lovely day. Aodhan and his father had made the decision to leave the surf shop closed for the day, since many of their employees had attended my parents' vow renewal and were probably still asleep. That meant we didn't have to deal with coworkers or customers as we entered the shop, grabbed what supplies we needed, and headed toward the boat waiting at the shop's private dock. Soon enough, we were speeding across the waves, because Aodhan drove the boat much the same way he drove his car.

"Are there speed limits on boats?" I asked.

"No. Why? Don't like feeling the wind in your hair?"

"I don't enjoy feeling like we're hurtling toward our doom," I muttered. Aodhan didn't say anything, but he did slow down. "Where are we going?"

"Not sure. I thought we'd find a nice spot and drop anchor for a while." He steered toward the Cliffs of Moher, and the imposing sea stack, Branaunmore. "Do you like it here?"

"Here is good." Honestly, all the water looked the same to me.

While Aodhan managed the boat's controls, I went to the rear and gazed at the vast expanse of water. It was so beautiful, and, thanks to the maps Grandfather had shown me, I knew that Kilstiffen lay a few kilometers off the coast of Ireland and deep below the ocean's surface, a magically protected city under the waves. While I contemplated the city down below, Aodhan came up behind me and embraced me.

"It's beautiful, isn't it?" I asked. The sea was a deep blue, which was a perfect contrast to the light, bright sky.

"Gorgeous," he said, as he dipped his head and nuzzled my neck.

"You're not even looking."

"Fine." Aodhan faced forward with his cheek pressed against mine. "The sea is beautiful, the waves are majestic, and this sky is positively poetic. Can I kiss you again?"

"All right," I said, then I twisted around and kissed him. For a moment, I worried we'd go over the side, but Aodhan's arms were strong. He'd never let me fall.

My bracelet caught on his shirt, and scratched me. "Ow," I said, as I examined my wrist. "Maybe I shouldn't have worn this."

Aodhan glanced at my skin. "Just a scratch," he said. "Want to go into the cabin?"

"I like it out here. We're all alone, yet I feel like we're part of everything."

"I understand," he began, then he looked at my wrist again, and frowned. "You're bleeding. Wait here, and I'll fetch a plaster."

I watched as Aodhan retreated into the cabin to grab the first aid kit. He was always taking care of me, whether I wanted him to or not, and I was well aware of how lucky I was to be with someone as kind and attentive as him. I also understood that his main reason for wanting to take the boat out was so we could talk about the future, and honestly, the thought of that just tied my stomach up in knots.

It wasn't that I didn't love Aodhan, because I did. I loved him so, so much. But yesterday he'd brought up marriage, and we were very young, and how was that a good idea? Then again, my mother had met Da the day after her eighteenth birthday, and married him less than a year later. And Kevin was only a few years older than me, and he seemed to be on track to marry Kelsey sooner rather than later. Perhaps merrows were supposed to marry young.

A puffin flew overhead, distracting me from my thoughts. I'd always loved the adorable little birds, with their snowy white breasts and brightly colored beaks. I rested my elbows on the edge of the boat's railing as I watched the bird fly toward the sea stack, and roost with his mates.

Suddenly, my wrist burned. I looked down, and saw a fat droplet of blood roll off my skin and splash into the sea below. The water went black and churned into a froth.

"Aodhan," I called. The black water reared up like a snake, and I took a step back.

"Aodhan," I screamed, but it was too late. The plume of dark water curled around my body and dragged me into the depths of the sea.

TRAPPED

A hacking noise roused me. A moment later, I realized that sound was coming from me as I coughed up seawater. I rolled onto my side, curled into the fetal position, and purged the rest of the water from my lungs. As soon as I had my breathing under control, I took in my surroundings.

I was lying on a cold, sandy floor, and it, and the walls and ceiling, appeared to be natural stone. A cave, then. Based on the many new aches spread across my back and legs, and that my hair and clothes were soaking wet, I deduced that I'd been thrown onto the floor after being fished out of the sea. But who had gotten me out of the water, and then put me here?

There was enough light for me to get a good look at my surroundings, and I dared to hope I was on land. When I sat up, and saw a bit more of the cave, my heart fell. There was an opening in the center of the cave's ceiling, but it was too high for me to reach, and I had no way to climb up to it. There was a faint blue shimmer across the opening, which reminded me of water. The fact that it wasn't rushing into the opening told me that magic was in play. However, that opening was also my sole source of light, so I had to be near the surface. Near the surface of what remained to be seen.

As I replayed my last memories before passing out, I realized that the bracelet I'd worn against Aodhan's better judgement had been the cause of my current predicament. It had scratched my wrist, my blood fell into the water, the water grabbed me, and now I was a prisoner in what appeared to be an undersea cave. Being that this bracelet had been presented to me by the council of lords, there were bigger schemes happening that just my kidnapping. Then I remembered the nearly identical cuff they'd given Kevin, and resolve settled across my shoulders like a cloak.

"You will not harm my brother," I said, just to hear my own voice. "I will get out of here, and you will be sorry."

"Don't count on it, little one."

For all that I'd hoped to never hear that voice again, I instantly recognized it. I turned around and saw Nahel, the wave dancer prince of Ker Ys and my former betrothed, watching me from the heretofore unnoticed mouth of the cave.

"Why am I here?" I demanded.

"Why, to become my wife," he replied. "You will be eighteen in what, a few days? Then you will be old enough for marriage."

"Manannán voided our betrothal," I said. "We are not getting married."

"Manannán isn't here," Nahel said. "I figure if I leave you in this cave for a while, you'll be so eager to get out of here, you'll leap into my bed."

"Think again," I snapped.

Nahel smirked. "We'll see, little one."

With that, he left, which was fantastic. What was not fantastic was that it was cold, and I was shivering in my wet clothes. I needed to find a way out of this cave, but first I had to get warm and dry. As I sang a few warming notes, I clutched my pearl pendant. The fact that Nahel hadn't taken it from me proved how foolish and arrogant he was, since this pearl was a direct line to my great-grandfather, Manannán mac Lir. As I sang, I told him I'd been kidnapped, that I was alone and scared and cold, and that Nahel was responsible. At my song's end, moments before my voice gave out, I asked Manannán to make sure my brother was safe, and to tell Aodhan I loved him.

Sad Villain Monologue

I'd spent the last few hours in a dark corner of the cave, coaxing the shadows to conceal me with a few quiet notes as I waited for my vocal chords to return to full strength. My music teacher, Rose, had always described one's voice as a muscle, and like all muscles, they needed rest. I wanted to make sure mine was exceptionally strong, because the next time I sang, I would be escaping this hell.

Nahel had come by to taunt me a few times from the entrance across from where I was hiding, as much as one could hide within a cave with only one way in or out. An earlier exploration of the area taught me that the entrance was secured by a version of the magic that held the sea at bay overhead, which was good. My voice was strong, and I hoped that once I recovered, my songs punch straight through that magic. As for what lay beyond that barrier, I could only hope there was a path out of here.

A large part of that hope rested on help arriving in one form or another, the sooner the better. I was certain Manannán wouldn't abandon me, but I also didn't know where I was, or how long I'd been out after my initial abduction. For all I knew, I'd been taken days ago, and was now on the other side of the planet.

I clutched the pearl in my hand, and asked, "Manannán, where are you?"

"You're wasting your breath," Nahel said. He was back yet again. This time he was standing right in the entrance of my cave, and holding a tray. "You're too far from water. He'll never hear you."

"That's not true," I said, with more confidence than I felt. "There's water overhead!"

"Is there? How far up is it?" When I didn't answer, Nahel gestured toward the cave walls. "Why do you think we put you, a merrow, among all this stone? Certainly not so you could sneak off, or call for reinforcements."

As much as I hated to admit it, his explanation made sense. "Won't the lack of water make you weaker, too?"

"I have other abilities," he replied, then he held the tray toward me. "Are you hungry?"

"Yes," I admitted. Nahel made a quick motion with his left hand, and the magical field that kept me imprisoned dissipated. With it gone, I could smell the warm bread and bowl of soup sitting on the tray. My stomach rumbled, and I stood up to receive it.

"Start with the water," Nahel said, as he indicated a small clay cup. I claimed it and took a small sip. The water was cool and clean, and I felt a bit of the fog lift from my brain. Thirst quenched, I reached for the bread, but Nahel pulled back the tray.

"The water was a gift, little one," he said. "But you can trade for the rest."

"Trade what?" I demanded, assuming he wanted my pendant.

"I'll let you have the bread for a kiss. The soup, however, that will require something more."

I stared at him, one fist clenched while the other held the clay cup. I finished my water and set the empty cup on the tray. "I'd rather starve than touch you."

Nahel smirked. "We'll see how you feel tomorrow, little one."

After Nahel left with his stupid bread and soup, I sat with my back against the cave wall facing the entrance, and waited for sleep to come. It didn't, partly because the ambient light never changed. A constant bluish glow filtered in from the opening in the ceiling, making it not only difficult to sleep. It was also near impossible to judge the passage of time. And if that wasn't water overhead, how would Manannán ever hear me?

I heard footsteps outside the cave. I grabbed my runners—I'd taken them off so they and my socks would dry faster—and stuffed my feet into them. As I crouched in the shadows, I heard two men talking.

"The older one hasn't been captured yet?"

"No. We may have to send a company above in order to retrieve him."

"He was given the same bracelet?"

"Yes. They both received them at the same time."

"If he's not located by nightfall, make the arrangements and acquire him by any means necessary. We need to have both of the heirs in our custody for this to work."

The men kept walking, as my mind raced with what I'd heard. They'd obviously been referring to Kevin, and they were going to capture him and drag him down here. I moved so I was directly under the light filtering down from above, and held the bracelet the council had given me close to my face. Along the inner rim of the bracelet were several short, sharp gold wires. You'd never see them if you weren't looking, and they were placed in such a way that the wearer might not notice them. I certainly hadn't. Eventually, the wires would pierce the wearer's skin and blood would be drawn, and whatever spell was imbued into the bracelet would activate.

Based on what I'd overheard, Kevin's spell hadn't activated. That was good. What wasn't good was that people were being sent above to capture him regardless of whether or not the spell scented blood and fired. I absent mindedly rubbed my thumb across the bracelet's large, central aquamarine, and recalled that Kevin's cuff held an identical gem.

Like two halves of a whole.

Siblings.

Notes flowed out of my mouth as I sang to the bracelet, a wordless warning to my brother. Would he hear me? These cuffs were created by magic and tied to us both, so I had to hope my song would reach him. As to whether or not he would understand my warning, again, all I had was hope.

"What was that song about?" asked a man. I recognized his voice as one of the two who'd walked by the cave earlier.

I faced the entrance, and saw a tall, thin man with a dark complexion and bright green eyes. He carried a metal-topped cane under his arm, which made me think it was more for show than mobility. He was wearing an ornate suit reminiscent of a formal military uniform, though I didn't recognize what country it was from. Not surprising, since I was mainly familiar with surface countries, and based on my circumstances, this man was obviously from below.

"What are you going to do with me?" I asked.

"I'm not really sure," he admitted. "Our plans hinge on having both you and your brother. With just you, I'm not sure they're viable."

"Why tell me that?" I demanded; if he thought his sad villain monologue was going to sway me to his cause, he had another thing coming. "Do you think if you're honest and bare your heart, I'll help you?"

"You asked me a question, and I answered it truthfully," he said with a shrug. "Most would appreciate that." As he moved, the light caught the bridge of his nose, and I saw it was crooked. That, coupled with his striking green eyes that matched Nahel's, told me who was behind my kidnapping.

"You're Gradlon's brother, Corentin," I said, and he nodded.

"You're smart like your mother," Corentin said. "I wonder what other traits you two share?"

"Our tempers, for one," I said. "When I tell her you're the one that took me, she'll probably kill you, unless she has my da finish the beating he started years ago in Kilstiffen."

Corentin pursed his lips, as his hand strayed toward his nose. "That beating, if you can call it that, is why you're here now."

"Bit late for revenge, don't you think?"

"Watch your mouth," he said quietly. "I may be tempted to do to you what your father did to me."

"You'd hit me, defenseless little me? You're lamer than I thought," I taunted. "You're just like your stupid nephew, can't stand that you didn't get the girl. What, don't you feel manly after—"

Magic crackled as pain exploded across the side of my face. Corentin had come into the cave so quickly I hadn't seen him move, and he'd backhanded me across my mouth. Tears sprang from my eyes as I stumbled back and fell to the floor.

"Do not try my patience," Corentin said, his words punctuated by blows to my arms and head. I rolled away from him, and he began hitting my back with his cane. "I've very little left!"

"How will your people feel about you hitting me?" I demanded, as scuttled out of his reach. "A queen with a black eye hardly garners sympathy!"

Corentin threw back his head and laughed. "You thought you were my prize? Nahel wants you, but I could care less what becomes of you."

"What do you want?" I asked.

"Kilstiffen," he replied. "And I'll destroy you and your useless brother in order to get it."

He turned on his heel and stalked away from my tiny cave, while I lay on the floor and tried to get my breathing under control. My head and back were in agonizing pain and my breath came in short gasps, but I had to push past all of that and think. The enchanted cuff had been given to me by the council of lords, and they wanted Grandfather to abdicate. Now Corentin admitted that he wanted Kilstiffen for himself, and that he will use me in any way possible to get it. Images of what that could mean flashed behind my eyes. I doubled over and retched at the thought, as the convulsions shot pain down my neck and around my ribs.

One thing was certain. I had to get out of this cave.

ESCAPE

After Corentin departed, no one approached my cave for some time, which was nice. Unfortunately, the blue light overhead remained as bright as ever. That either meant that the light was artificial, or I was losing all concept of time. Perhaps both of those things were true.

My solitude didn't last nearly long enough. While my body was still throbbing in pain from Corentin's tantrum, Nahel returned to taunt me. He regaled me with stories of what our wedding would be like, and how all the kingdoms would attend and shower us with gifts. When I didn't respond, he told me what he had planned for our wedding night. I nearly retched at his vile, detailed descriptions.

By what I thought was my third day of captivity, the various pains in my body had subsided to a dull ache. Being that Corentin wore a handful of rings, my face had gotten scratched as well as bruised, but without a mirror I didn't know how bad the damage was. I could feel plenty of scabs, though. Add to that the aches in my back, shoulders, and left hip, which I'd fallen on after he'd hit me, and all the aches from when I'd first been tossed into the cave, and I was little more than a bloody bruise. At least my feet were uninjured, and I fully planned on running out of here.

Worst of all, I was starving. My stomach was so empty it hurt, and it felt like I hadn't eaten in days, possibly longer. Probably longer, since I had no real notion of how long I'd been a prisoner. To distract myself from my hunger pangs, I made a weapon.

The traitorous bracelet that brought me here was made of gold, which is a very soft metal, and I was surrounded by rocks. No one had swept out this cave in quite some time—really, why would anyone do that?—and there were many smaller stones scattered about. I gathered them up and used a song to coax the metal to wrap itself around the rocks. By the time I heard footsteps outside the cave again, I had a gold and stone ball that fit in the palm of my hand. I wouldn't be able to throw it very far, but I could crack someone on the head and cause a fair bit of damage, and make a run for it. That is, run until I collapsed of starvation, or exhaustion, or pain, or all of those at once.

The footsteps paused in the corridor. I flattened myself against the wall next to the entrance, my weapon held aloft. Magic popped and sizzled as the barrier over the entrance dissolved, and the owner of the footsteps entered. It was Nahel, bearing another tray of food.

"Little one," he called, as he looked around the cave for me. "Are you in the mood to be a bit nicer to me today? I have a good, hot meal for you."

I stepped out from my hiding spot and thrust the heavy ball into Nahel's back, right over his kidney. The air whooshed out of him as he bent over and dropped the tray with a clatter. I brought the ball down on the back of his head, and knocked him out cold.

I stood next to Nahel's prone form, panting and sweating and was that more bread and soup on the tray? Most of the soup had spilled out of the bowl, but I grabbed it and drank what was left. That done, I snatched the bread and stuffed it into the front pocket of my sweatshirt, and ran into the corridor. There was light at one end, but I heard at least two guards talking to each other. Taking my chances, I turned the other way and plunged into darkness.

A torch flared, and the guards saw me.

"Stop her," one shouted, as they began pursuit. I glanced over my shoulder; what I'd thought were two guards were actually five. As I pushed myself to run harder, missiles flew past my body and struck the guards. One by one they fell, then an arm shot out and dragged me to a halt.

"Meri," a man said. "Come with me."

"How do you know my name?" I demanded, then I opened my mouth to sing. He sang first, and stole my voice. I felt the notes leave my throat as I stared at this man who knew my name, but who I knew nothing about.

No, that wasn't true. I knew he was a merrow, and based on the slingshot shoved into his belt, he'd felled all five of the guards behind me. Neither of those things automatically made him a friend.

"Scáthach sent me," he whispered. He released my arm and held his hands out, palms up, as he stepped back. His left hand held a small, glowing stone between his thumb and palm, and it cast his face in a bluish hue. "I'll get you out of here, but we need to be fast and quiet."

I tapped my throat. Understanding, he sang again, and I felt my voice restored. "Who are you?"

"A friend." He glanced at my feet. I was glad I'd remembered to put my runners back on. "We're going to have to climb a bit. Are you up for it?"

"This climb will take me to the surface?"

"Eventually. At first, we'll go lower, where I have a hidey hole."

"How can I know if Scáthach truly sent you?" I asked. "Prove it."

"I don't have a password or a secret handshake, if that's what you're asking." He looked down the tunnel the way I'd come from, and frowned. "I can tell you that she's the second deadliest warrior born of Kilstiffen."

That was the truth, but I remained rooted in place. "That lot won't stay out for long," the man said, when I didn't move. "I'll answer all your questions, I swear it, but we need to move."

"All right." I didn't trust this man, but he seemed to know my aunt, which meant he also knew my mother. Going with him was my best option, for now. "Lead the way."

Our trek through the tunnels was more than a quick climb. At first, the tunnel sloped upward, and I dared to hope I'd find an offshoot that would lead me to the surface. I never found such an escape route. Instead, we trudged on and on through the darkness with only the one small glowing stone to light our way.

We weren't moving very quickly, but I was in agony. The entire left side of my body throbbed in pain, my back ached as if someone had twisted my spine into a knot, and my cheek and jaw were sore. I was not doing well, and I desperately needed to rest.

"Can we stop soon?" I asked.

"Not much farther, now," the man said. "I don't want to risk stopping until you're safe."

"Who made these tunnels?" I asked, mostly to distract myself from the pain. "Or are they natural?"

"They've been here for eons," he replied. "All of the sea kingdoms are linked by these tunnels. We've enlarged and improved them over time, but as far as I know, the caves were here long before we were."

"You seem to know these caves well."

"Aye. This isn't the first rescue mission I've gone on. Here we are." He made a sharp left. I followed, and found myself standing in yet another cave, though this one was set up like a sitting room. It was about the size of my dining room, and I could see a cot pushed against one wall, and crates stacked against another.

"Do you live down here?" I asked.

"No," he replied, as he pulled a heavy curtain over the entrance. That done, he set down the glowing stone and turned on an electric lantern. "This is more of a waystation. You can rest up here, tend your wounds, and then we'll be on."

"Tend my wounds? Do you have a first aid kit?"

He cocked his head to the side. "You can heal yourself, with your voice. Has no one taught you how?"

"Um, no. I've only recently become aware of being half merrow." My stomach growled, and I remembered the bread in my pocket. I withdrew it, and held it toward him. "I took this from my cell. Want half?"

"You need it more than me." He was right about that. As I tore off a piece and shoved it into my mouth, he set up a folding table and chairs. "Here, sit for a bit. I've got some food and water in my stores. It's not great, but it'll be a fair sight better than being hungry."

I sat, and ate my bread while he located a pot and tin of soup. He set everything up over a small camping stove, then he found a kettle and filled it from a canteen. "Tea?"

"Please." I watched as he set the kettle next to the pot, and got two tin cups ready with tea bags. "It seems like you're in this waystation rather often."

"More often than I would like." He claimed the chair across from me, and nodded toward my shoulder. "I see you've met Talia."

"How could you know that?"

"That's her embroidery. I'd recognize it anywhere."

I glanced at my shoulder. Talia had repaired the holes ripped into my sweatshirt by the gancanagh by embroidering seashells onto the fabric with golden thread, that much was true. According to my mother, when those in Kilstiffen made a repair, they aimed to make the item better than it had been before it had been damaged.

"How do you know Talia?" I asked.

"She looked after me when I was small," he replied. "Used to call me and my sisters the three wee hellions. Your mother was the worst of all of us," he added, and I as I took in his blond hair and eyes as blue as Niamh's, I suddenly understood who he was.

"Are you Oscar?" I asked, and he nodded. "My mother's been looking for you."

"Aoife knows no one can find me, not unless I want to be found. Which isn't often," he added, then the kettle whistled. While he fixed our tea, he said, "However, there are ways to get messages to me. When Scáthach told me how you'd been dragged overboard, I left at once."

"How did she even know that?"

"A man told her," Oscar replied. "He was on the boat with you, saw you go over. Aodhan, was his name?"

"Yes. Aodhan." I squeezed my eyes shut, but my mind saw fit to show me images of Aodhan looking on in horror as I was dragged away from him. "Can we send him a message?"

"We can, but not from here," Oscar said. "Soon."

"Why did they send you after me?" I asked, wondering why Scáthach or my mother hadn't come themselves instead of sending someone I'd never met. "No offense, for I do appreciate the rescue, but I am curious."

"Simple. I was closest." Oscar set the two mugs of tea on the table. "Sorry, I don't have any milk."

"This is perfect. Thank you, truly." I held the mug with both of my hands, and let the warmth seep into my fingers. "How did you know where to look for me?"

Oscar's face darkened. "That other rescue I mentioned? It was Aoife. The bastard MacCreehy captured her some years back, and put her in chains with a collar that kept her voice subdued. It took me months to find her, but find her I did. I broke Aoife out of her chains and got her to our sister in Evonium."

I remembered Mama telling me how she'd been imprisoned in a cave, and had missed her meeting with Da. She'd been despondent afterward, and assumed he would never forgive her. She'd also been wrong, because my father loved her so much he would forgive her anything.

"And she was held here?" I asked.

"Nearby. The council has long used this network of caves as a prison block."

I pulled my pendant out of my shirt. "I tried to contact Manannán mac Lir with this pearl, but I was told there's so much rock down here that he would never hear me. Is that true?"

"Aye, that's the truth," Oscar said. "Once a merrow's been stuck down here, so far from any type of water, their voice wanes, and soon enough they're nearly helpless." Oscar got up and turned off the camp stove, then he ladled the soup into a bowl.

"Here we are," he said, as he set the bowl before me. "Hang on, I've got spoons around here somewhere."

Oscar found me a spoon, and I investigated the soup. It was an overly salty minestrone, but at that moment I didn't care. It was the best soup I'd ever had, and I finished every drop. Afterward, full of warm soup and hot tea, I felt my eyes closing.

"Come on now, Meri," Oscar said, as he helped me up. "Have a bit of a lie down."

"But we need to escape," I mumbled.

"Aye, and we won't get very far until you've had some rest." He got me onto the cot and pulled a blanket over me. "You're safe here. I won't let anyone hurt you."

"I wish Aodhan was here," I said, then I passed out.

BACK TO THE MERMAID'S CAVE

"**M**eri. Meri. Time to go."

I opened my eyes, and saw Oscar crouched beside me. "I'm still so tired."

"I know you are, but the council's guards swept through here around an hour ago," he said. "The concealment held, but I don't want to risk us being found."

"Concealment?" I sat up, and put my feet on the floor. "You're hiding us magically?"

"The spell is woven into the tarp over the door." He pointed toward the door's covering, and I saw filaments of gold in the dark fabric. "Times past these spells were called glamours. They make you overlook things, but if anyone reached out and touched the door, they'd feel a length of cloth instead of a stone wall."

"That's a neat trick," I said, then I stood and hissed in pain. My feet, my legs... everything just hurt. Oscar frowned at me, then he pointed toward a curtained off area at the back of the room.

"There's a privy there, and water for washing," he said. "Get yourself together, and I'll get us something to eat."

I entered the privy, which was a rather primitive affair. It was, however, loads better than the bucket I'd been provided in the cave. The water turned out to be a small stream that snaked down the rock wall and emptied into a shallow pool. Once I was as refreshed as I was going to get, I emerged and saw Oscar bustling around the camp stove.

"Sit," he said, as he jerked his chin toward the table. "We'll have a bit of breakfast, and one lesson in healing, then we move."

"Want me to make the tea?" I asked, my battered hands itching with the need to do something. "Or anything else?"

"Tea's ready." Oscar set the mugs on the table, along with a packet of biscuits. "Take a moment, eat your fill. You need strength in order to sing."

I nodded, and tore open the packet. The biscuits were a bit stale, but I didn't mind. My raging hunger meant I would happily eat all the stale biscuits in the world.

"I know you've got a lot of pain," Oscar said, after I'd wolfed down my fifth biscuit. "Focus on a small injury, and I'll teach you how to heal it."

"Why a small one?" I asked, since I had some rather large injuries that could use a bit of attention.

"We don't have a lot of time, and once you know how to heal small wounds, you can work toward the bigger ones," he replied. "Where would you like to begin?"

I held out my wrist, and showed Oscar the cut that started all of this. "The council gave me a bracelet. It cut me here, and my blood dripped into the sea. That was how the magic knew to grab me." I took a breath; recounting that had been more intense than I'd anticipated. "I'd like to do away with this cut first."

"Bastards," Oscar muttered, then he moved to take my hand. "May I?"

"Yes. Of course."

Oscar cradled my wrist in his palm, and set his glowing stone next to it. "You know how fabric tears? Skin tears in much the same way. I want you to think about fabric tearing, the pulling and the pressure and then the big rip, and what all of that sounds like."

"All right." I recalled an incident from when I was small, and Kevin and I had inadvertently torn the kitchen tablecloth in half. We'd been our own version of wee hellions. "Got it."

"Now sing it, but in reverse."

I stared at Oscar and then at the cut on my wrist. Could it really be that easy? I imagined the cruel sound of fabric rending, and picked the notes apart one by one. Slowly, I strung them together like a string of pearls, but in the opposite order. By the third time I'd sung the notes, the pain in my wrist was gone. Amazingly, so was the cut.

"It worked," I said, as I marveled at my unmarred skin.

"Didn't you believe me?" Oscar said, with a grin that reminded me of Mama. "Grab the canteens and get them filled. Let's get moving."

I filled two canteens from the stream in the rear of the room, then Oscar claimed one as he handed me the half-empty packet of biscuits, and we were on our way. This time, the tunnels we traversed either remained level or sloped upward. Hopefully, I would see the sun again soon.

"So, who's Aodhan?" Oscar asked. When I didn't reply readily, he continued, "I know you were on the boat with him, and you called out for him in your sleep."

"Did I?" I couldn't remember any of last night's dreams, which was probably for the best. "He's my best friend, my partner in everything." I paused, and added, "He asked me to marry him."

"Did you say yes?"

"We went out on the boat to talk about it." My throat tensed and my eyes burned, but tears didn't come. "We never got the chance."

"Never fear, Meri," Oscar said. "You'll have that talk when you see him again."

Oscar's confidence bolstered my own. "So, why are you always sneaking around down here?" I asked. "Grandfather made it seem like you were living the easy life in Tir na nÓg."

"You're referring to when I was banished below?" Oscar countered. "And there's nothing easy about being in Tir na nÓg."

"Sorry. I didn't meant to be insensitive."

"It's all right. As for why I was banished, I defied the council one too many times. My father's options were to either punish me, or send me below to hide out with my mother's people."

"That council is made up of devils," I said. "They're trying to shove Grandfather off the throne, and they tried to make my brother and I marry the twins from Ker Ys."

"Don't worry about the king. He's not called Steinar the Immoveable for nothing. As for Ker Ys, they've been in the council's pocket for years."

"Do you know why?" I asked. "Their king, Gradlon, is always acting as if Kilstiffen owes him in some way. We don't, do we?"

"We certainly do not," Oscar said. "Gradlon's a greedy and jealous man, but more importantly, he can't run his city to save his life. After years of him ruining alliances and squandering resources, Ker Ys is the poorest of the sea kingdoms. He probably wants you and Kevin to marry his children so he can steal your dowries."

I remembered when Da told me about the dowry Mama received upon their marriage. It was paid in gold bars, and they were so heavy it took ten men to carry them above. "The more I learn about Gradlon, the farther I wish to be from him."

"On that, we do agree." Oscar glanced at me. "I assume you and your brother declined these marriages?"

"We did. Immediately. Later on, Manannán mac Lir himself voided them."

"That must have pissed Gradlon off."

"I'm sure it did. Right before that happened, I stole all his precious fancy salt from beneath Ker Ys. I'm sure he didn't like that, either."

Oscar doubled over in laughter. "Oh, Meri, that's priceless," he said, as he leaned on the cave wall to keep from tumbling over. "You're definitely one of the hellions, and I bet your brother is, too. What did you do with all that salt?"

"I used it against Donn Dumhach, and then I defeated an ankou that had attacked my school."

My uncle nodded approvingly. "Yes, you're definitely Aoife's child. All of us hellions are as fierce as the warriors of old, but Aoife has always burned brighter."

Grandfather often referred to Mama as his youngest, fiercest child. "Why are you three all fired up? Or are Kilstiffen's heirs traditionally warriors?"

Oscar shrugged. "We love our home, and our family, and we fight for what we love. Isn't that what you've been doing? Surely you didn't tangle with Donn Dumhach on a lark."

"I wouldn't call it a tangle. He was Aodhan's stepfather."

"Ah. It always cuts a bit deeper when the villain turns out to be family, either by blood or by circumstance."

The way he said that made me pause. "Who's the villain in our family?"

"No one blood related, and the incident I mentioned happened long ago," he replied, then we reached the end of a tunnel. Another opening was set in the center of the wall, the floor level with Oscar's shoulders. "Here, I'll give you a boost up."

I set my foot in Oscar's hands, and he heaved me into the opening. I scrambled up into the next tunnel, then I heard Oscar singing as he magically lifted himself into the tunnel behind me.

"You seem to know quite a few tricks," I said.

"Have to down here," he replied. We moved down the tunnel, which opened up into a large cavern. There was water on the cave floor, which looked clear but smelled awful. Hanging from the ceiling was a massive and familiar stalactite.

"I've been in this before," I said. "When Aodhan and I were searching for my mother, we came through here. We met a stone merrow."

"You've met our cousin Tallulah, then?" Oscar asked, then we heard a loud crack that came from the opposite side of the cavern.

"Down," Oscar bellowed. I flung myself into the rank water as a volley of arrows sailed overhead and clattered against the cave formations. Across the cavern were a dozen warriors holding crossbows, and shields that depicted a white horse galloping atop the sea.

"Who are they?" I demanded.

"Not friends," Oscar replied, as if that wasn't obvious. The warriors loosed another volley of arrows. Oscar sang, and I watched as the air thickened. The arrows didn't get within a few metres of us, and splashed harmlessly into the pools on the cave's floor.

Suddenly, all the lights went on full blast and rocks and tools begin raining down on the bad guys from up above. After a moment, I figured out that the missiles were coming from the viewing platform. Wondering if there were more foes behind us, I looked up, and could hardly believe my eyes.

Aodhan was there.

"Get down here," I yelled, because isn't yelling at the man who came to rescue you the proper way to greet him. Instead of following my instruction, Aodhan kept throwing rocks at our attackers.

"Get up here instead," he yelled. "Mer, we've got to get out of here!"

He was right—Aodhan and I weren't warriors, and Oscar couldn't hold off the rest on his own. I began to say as much, when Oscar paused for breath. In that moment of silence, and a stray arrow zipped through the air and pierced Oscar's calf.

He went down hard, his blood darkening the water on the cave floor. As I rushed to help Oscar, and get him behind a boulder or pile of rocks to shield him, Aodhan came up beside me.

"Meri," Aodhan said, then he saw Oscar. "Let me take him. Cover me."

I had no idea what "cover me" meant. Aodhan grabbed Oscar under his arms, and dragged him behind a stand of boulders. I sang to thicken the air as Oscar did, and hopefully prevent the arrows from reaching us. At the last moment before my voice gave out, I dove behind the boulders.

And straight into Aodhan's arms.

"Meri," he murmured, as he folded me into his arms. "Christ, Mer, I was terrified I'd never see you again."

"I missed you so much." I held him so tightly my arms hurt, but I didn't care about the pain. After everything that had happened down in the caves, I might never let go of him.

Aodhan stroked his hand down my hair. "Are you all right?"

"I'm okay," I said, which wasn't really the truth. I was battered and bloody and despite the food Oscar had fed me, I was still in imminent danger of starvation. Somehow, none of that mattered, not as long as Aodhan was holding me. "How did you know to come here?"

"Scáthach said Oscar would bring you to the mermaid's cave," he replied, then he drew back and frowned once he got a closer look at my face. I must have looked as awful as I felt. "What the hell happened to you?"

"A lot," I said, then Oscar groaned. "I'll tell you everything. Promise."

Aodhan nodded, then he focused on the arrow in Oscar's leg. "I take it you're Oscar?"

"I am. Hang on." Oscar grabbed the arrow and yanked it out of his leg, causing a waterfall of blood to pour out of his leg. Just as I was about to have a panic attack, he sang to heal himself. Before my eyes, the blood on his calf disappeared.

"You're the one that called Scáthach?" Oscar asked, once he was healed up.

"That's right." Aodhan stood, and looked past the boulders. "What should we do about that lot?"

"We need to keep them from following us," Oscar said. "Their regalia marks them as foot soldiers from Ker Ys. They're most likely here to recapture Meri, and go above to take Kevin, too."

I stood next to Aodhan, my gaze fixed on the Ker Ysian warriors. "I will kill every last one of them before I allow them to lay a hand on my brother," I muttered, then I sang.

No. I *screamed*.

The earth rumbled, then the massive stalactite broke free from the cavern's ceiling and crashed to the ground. I covered my face, shielding my eyes from the rock shards flying about the chamber. Once the dust settled I lowered my arm, and saw that the fallen stalactite had cut the Ker Ysians off completely.

"We're safe from them, for the moment." I said, as I offered Oscar a hand. "Let's get out of here."

"You two go up to the surface," Oscar said, as he stood. "I'm going back down to the tunnels and on to Evonium. Once you've recovered, meet us there."

"Us?" I repeated, then I glanced at his leg. There was no evidence remaining of the arrow that had pierced his calf, or the injury it caused. "Will you be all right?"

Oscar set his hand on my shoulder. "I will. Aodhan, thanks for looking out for my niece. See you both soon?"

"Soon," Aodhan said. They grasped forearms, then Oscar slipped into the shadows.

"Come on," Aodhan said. "Let's get out of here."

HOME

Aodhan and I were quiet as we climbed up the rock cut stairs and made our way out of the cave and back to the surface. I was so exhausted I could barely put one foot in front of the other, and the fight against the Ker Ysians had affected both of us. We didn't see any other patrons exploring the caves, or any employees. At the time I was grateful, but when we exited to the car park, I learned the true reason why. It was nighttime, and the caves were closed.

"What time is it?" I asked.

Aodhan withdrew his phone. "About two in the morning," he said, then he brought the phone to his ear. "I have her."

"Who is that?" I demanded.

"Kevin," Aodhan replied, then he handed me his phone. I stared at it for a moment, then I took the device.

"Hi."

"Meri," Kevin said, as I gasped. My brother was safe, and that meant nearly as much to me as my own safety. "Goddamnit Meri, I am so happy to hear your voice!"

"It was the bracelet," I said. "They wanted to capture both of us. There's a spell in it, and a bunch of spikes on the inside that will cut you. Don't wear it!"

"I haven't been. You're all right?"

"No, not really," I replied, then I saw Aodhan watching me. "But I will be."

"All right. I'll tell everyone that you're safe. Call me after you get some rest, and don't leave Aodhan's sight."

"I won't. Promise."

I handed the phone back to Aodhan. He said a few words to Kevin, then he pocketed the phone and pulled me into his arms.

"Careful," I said. "I must smell awful."

"I don't care," he said. His arms were so tight the bruises and scrapes on my arms and back were howling in pain, but I didn't mention it. I just hugged Aodhan back. "I've been waiting here for days, ever since Scáthach said Oscar would bring you out this way. The staff thinks I'm mental."

"Days?" I pulled back, and met his eyes. "How long have I been below?"

"Six days."

"Oh." I swallowed, wholly unprepared to deal with that information. "I suppose that's why I'm so hungry."

His brows pinched. "No one fed you?"

"I had a bit of bread, and Oscar gave me some soup and biscuits."

Aodhan smoothed back my stiff hair. "Let's go home, and get you some food. I'll tell you everything that happened on the way."

We got into Aodhan's car, and he sped down the dark, winding roads. After a few minutes, I realized we were driving toward the centre of town, rather than toward my place. "We're heading to the shop?"

"No one's at your house," he replied. "Your parents went on to Evonium, and Kevin and Kelsey went down to Kilstiffen. Actually, everyone is probably in Evonium by now." Aodhan glanced at me. "Your aunt has an army up there."

"Does she?" I asked, but then I had known about the training academy. "What happened after I went over?"

"I almost jumped in after you, but you were taken by magic." His voice caught. I reached over and took his hand. "The water, it stood up and grabbed you."

"I'm glad you didn't follow," I said. "You could have died."

He squeezed my hand. "Since swimming after you was out of the question, I called Kevin. He roused your ma. Your aunt was still at your place, and she knew how to send a message to Oscar. He found you soon enough?"

"He found me yesterday," I replied. "They kept me in a cave. Nahel was there. I knocked him out and fled into the tunnels. That was where Oscar found me."

"Did you kill Nahel? Please say no, so I can beat him senseless."

"I didn't stop to check on him. Right after I got past him, I ran into Oscar."

Aodhan brought my hand to his mouth and kissed my knuckles. "I wanted to go below and find you myself, but your ma said Oscar was the best person to get you out. Also, we have a full on war happening with Ker Ys. Now that we know Nahel was there, I'm sure things will heat up."

"Good," I snapped. "Gradlon's brother, Corentin, was there, too. He said he wants Kilstiffen, and he'd use me and Kevin to get it. And

Nahel said... he said..." I paused to get myself under control. "He told me, in absolutely disgusting detail, what he would do to me, once he married me."

A string of curses issued forth from Aodhan. "Did he touch you?"

"No. He stood outside my cell and taunted me. He never set foot in it, except once to give me water, and the time I knocked him out. Corentin's the one that beat me."

Aodhan went still. "Corentin hit you."

"Yes. He did." I saw Aodhan's jaw working. "Don't worry. If you say you want to kill him, I won't be mad."

"Good, because I am going to destroy him."

We reached the surf shop, and I followed Aodhan upstairs to the apartment. I hadn't been there for a few weeks, since we'd been busy getting the garden ready for my parents' vow renewal at my house. When we turned on the lights, the first thing I noticed was a new door past the kitchenette.

"You replaced the door to the storage room?" I asked.

"Remember when I told you I was fixing the place up? I decided to turn the storage area into a proper bedroom. There's furniture and everything, but it still needs a bit of work."

I nodded, then I caught sight of myself in the entryway's mirror. The bruises on my cheek had faded to a mottled green, my many cuts were scabbed over, and my hair had dried blood and cave slime living in it. "I look like a corpse. Can I... Can I have a shower?"

"Of course. I'll put together something to eat while you're in there."

I nodded again, and entered the bathroom. I tried to remove my runners, but my fingers were bloody and battered from climbing through the caves, and I couldn't untie the laces. Leaving the shoes for the moment, I tried to turn on the shower, but pain in my hands and shoulders prevented me moving the knob. Defeated, I sat on the toilet. If I couldn't turn on the water, I also couldn't remove my sweatshirt, and between the excruciating pain and my near total exhaustion, I was one moment away from a full breakdown.

I opened the door, and called, "Aodhan?"

"Yeah, love?"

"Can you come in here, please?"

He was in the doorway a moment later. "What do you need?"

"I can't get my shoes off, and I can't turn on the water, and..." I swallowed my shame, and asked, "Can you help me get undressed, and then help me take a shower?"

"Um. Yeah. Hang on."

Aodhan reached into the shower and started the water, then he knelt at my feet and removed my runners and socks. That done, he helped me stand, then he went behind me in order to get the rest of my clothes off. I supposed him staring at my back was his concession for modesty. Once everything was off, he tested the water's temperature, and pulled back the shower curtain.

"Ready?"

"Yeah."

He steadied my elbows as we got into the tub. Aodhan stayed behind me as he used the handheld sprayer to wet down my hair. "Is it too warm?" he asked.

"No. It's good."

He grunted, then he set the sprayer aside and began washing my hair. "Might have to shampoo you twice."

"Three times, maybe." I closed my eyes, and tried to lose myself in the sensations of warm water rushing over me, and Aodhan's hands rubbing my scalp. He was careful with my snarled mass of hair, and the gentle massage nearly put me to sleep.

"Turn around, so I can rinse you."

I did, and set my hands on Aodhan's chest to steady myself... His bare chest. I opened my eyes, and realized he was also naked. That made sense. After all, who wears clothes in the shower? I certainly didn't. And now Aodhan and I were in the shower together. Naked.

Since I couldn't deal with any of that, I slid my arms around Aodhan's waist and laid my cheek against his chest. He paused in his soaping and rinsing, and draped his arms around my shoulders.

"Are you doing okay?" he asked. "Want to stop?"

"I'd rather scrub off the rest of the cave slime," I replied. Aodhan grabbed a washcloth and container of shower gel, and started on my back. He was thorough, and gentle, and with the exception of where I leaned against him for support, he never touched me, save with the washcloth. When he got down to my feet, he kept his gaze on my toes, and never even tried to steal a glance at my body.

Every time I think I couldn't possibly love him more, he goes and does something gallant like this.

"I believe we're done," Aodhan declared, then he shut off the water and handed me a towel. While I blotted my hair, he found a robe and helped me put it on. Then he picked me up and carried me out of the bathroom.

"What's all this?" I asked.

"If you're too tired to stand up in the shower, you're too tired to walk across the apartment," he replied. He brought me into the bedroom, and set me down on the edge of the bed. "Want me to comb out your hair?"

"I can manage," I said. "Thank you. I don't know what I'd do without you."

He leaned over and kissed me. "You'll never have to know. Get a shirt or something from my dresser, then get under the blankets and stay warm. I'll bring you some food from the kitchen."

Once I was alone, I stood and shed the robe, and was immediately chilled. I recalled that the shop's heater was on a timer, and didn't turn on until ten. I pulled the blanket over me, intending to take a moment to rest and warm up. As soon as my head landed on the pillow, I was asleep.

My rumbling stomach roused me. It wasn't as bad as it had been below, when Corentin and Nahel were trying to starve me into compliance. Thank the gods for Oscar, and his stash of tinned soup and stale biscuits. Still, I could do with a full breakfast sooner rather than later. As I thought about plates heaped with scrambled eggs and steaming cups of coffee, my stomach rumbled again. I set my hand on it to quell it, and found Aodhan's arm tight around my waist.

I rolled over, and watched him sleep. As bad as things were below, never once had I worried I'd never see Aodhan again. I knew that he would either send someone after me, or find me himself, and that was exactly what had happened. Aodhan was constant, and reliable, and I believed in him more than anything.

No, that wasn't true. I believed in us. Together, we could do anything.

I noticed his bare chest. Curious, I stroked my hand down his side, and discovered he was just as naked as I was. I didn't feel a drop of shame or embarrassment, since I'd divested myself of both of those emotions while we were in the shower together. Now, I just wanted to stay here with him for as long as possible.

A familiar chime sounded from behind me. I rolled away from Aodhan, and found my phone lying on the bedside table. I had over a hundred notifications waiting for my attention, and dozens of voice mails.

"I've never been so popular in all my life," I muttered.

"A lot of those are from me," Aodhan said, his voice raspy, then he set his hand on my back. "Christ, Mer, when I saw your back in the shower, I was hoping most of this was dirt. Are all these bruises from Corentin?"

"Not all of them." I set down the phone, and turned to face him. "Why did you call so many times?" I asked, since he was well aware my phone had been left behind on the boat.

"I needed to hear your voice." He stroked his hand down my neck, coming to rest on my shoulder. "After your ma and Scáthach sent Oscar after you, the waiting was terrible. I needed to know you were okay, but I knew there was no way for Oscar to get a message out without compromising himself. So I called your phone, and listened to your voice mail greeting."

"Did you leave me messages?"

"Yeah. They're awful. Probably should delete them without listening to them."

"What if I want to hear them all?" I asked, as I moved closer to him. Underneath the covers, my toes touched the tops of his feet. "What if I want to keep them, and treasure them, and listen to them whenever I need to feel loved?"

"You'll always be loved," he said, then he propped himself up on his elbow and gazed at me as if I was his world. "Always."

"Did you soundproof this room?"

"Not yet. Why?"

"I'd like to finish that conversation we started a week ago."

NEW SHOES

"I missed my birthday."

Aodhan and I were in bed again. Earlier, we'd taken another shower, and had something to eat, then he gave me two paracetamol and sent me to lie down. Since I didn't want to be alone, he came with me. Now I was curled up against his side, with my cheek against his throat and my hand resting on his chest over his heart.

"I thought you never cared for celebrating your birthday," he said, as he stroked my hair.

"I was hoping this year would be different." I glanced up at him. "What was it like?"

"Not good," he replied. "Your parents didn't do well at all. It was when they made the decision to go to Kilstiffen."

"What do you mean, they didn't do well?"

"Your Ma was furious that she'd already missed so many of your birthdays, and now she missed yet another. She ended screaming and raging out in the garden all day. She even went at one of the apple trees with her sword, and nearly broke the blade."

I remembered Mama telling me about how she stabbed things when she was upset. "And Da?"

"He was the opposite. Being that he has spent every one of your birthdays with you, he was despondent. My dad and I worried he'd turn to whiskey, so we hid all the leftover bottles. Wine, too."

"That was smart," I muttered. Da's drinking to excess had started when he was separated from Mama, and feared she would never return. "What time is it?"

"Almost nine," Aodhan replied. I rolled over and grabbed my phone, and called Da. He picked up on the first ring.

"Meri?"

"Da! Da, are you all right?"

"I should be asking you that. Kevin told us you were safe, but he didn't say much else."

"I didn't really tell him anything else. But he was right, I'm safe with Aodhan at the shop. Oscar, he found me."

"That Oscar is a good one." I heard Da moving around. "I've never been so worried in all my life, Meri girl. We're all up in Evonium. Will you and Aodhan be joining us here soon?"

"As soon as we can. I love you, Da. I can't wait to hug you."

"I love you too, Meri girl. Hang on, your ma wants to talk to you."

I heard whispering, then Mama had the phone. "Meri!"

"Mama! Mama, they held me near where you'd been imprisoned. Oscar told me how he got you out."

"I knew he would find you. Who held you?"

"Ker Ys was behind it all. Corentin seemed to be in charge. Nahel was there, too, but not Dahut or Gradlon. At least, I didn't see them."

"Bastards," she growled. "I'll flay them alive for this."

"Are we really at war?"

"We are now," she declared. "When are you leaving for Evonium?"

"Um, as soon as we can?" I glanced Aodhan. Unhelpfully, he shrugged.

"On your way here stay off the sea," Mama advised. "Drive north, all the way through to County Antrim. When you reach The Giant's Causeway, we'll send a bridge for you."

"Giant's Causeway, bridge," I repeated. "No sea."

"As soon as we're all together, we'll met up with Kilstiffen's forces. And, Meri girl, I'm so sorry I missed your birthday."

"It's okay. Once all of this is behind us, Da can make us a cake and we'll celebrate anyway."

"You are a treasure, my lamb. Never doubt that I love you will all of my heart."

"I love you, too, Mama."

We ended the call, then I tossed the phone aside and let Aodhan gather me against his chest. "Mama wants us to go to The Giant's Causeway. When we get there, she'll send us a bridge, and we'll take that to Evonium." I peeked up at him. "I have no idea how that's going to work."

"We'll know soon enough." He tightened his arms around me, but eased up when I winced. "You said Oscar taught you how to heal yourself?"

"He did, but I don't want to heal my injuries. Not all of them, not just yet. I want to stand there in front of Kilstiffen's army and show them exactly what Corentin did to me. I want everyone to know what a monster he is."

"Then what?"

"Then, as Mama said, we'll flay him alive."

I could have done with more rest, but I was far too wired to sleep. Since Aodhan had thrown my clothes into the washer right after we'd showered the first time, and then the dryer after we showered the second time, as soon as they were done, I got dressed. It was a bit odd to be wearing the same kit I'd had on for the past seven days, but it did include my favorite shorts and sweatshirt. At least everything was clean again, too. As for footwear, my runners were unfortunately done for.

"We should toss these," Aodhan said, as he gingerly lifted my runners by their laces. The combination of seawater, cave detritus, and whatever other dirt they'd come in contact with had destroyed them. "We've got tons of shoes and sandals down in the shop. Go have a look, and pick out a pair."

While Aodhan binned my shoes, I went down to the shop. Along the way, I noted that there wasn't a door separating the shop from the apartment, just the wide carpeted staircase. That didn't matter while the shop was closed, but what if Aodhan and I were upstairs *alone* during business hours and a customer wandered into the apartment? That would get awkward, fast. As I imagined talking myself out of that situation, Lorcan entered through the shop's front door.

"Um, hello," I said.

"Meri, we were worried about you, lass," Lorcan said. "Was it just the Ker Ysians that were after you, like Aoife thought? Not that they aren't plenty," he added.

"I don't think Donn was involved," I said, since that was what he really wanted to know. The surf shop was built above Donn Dumhach's abode, the legendary Tech Duinn. Lorcan was the last in a long line of guardians tasked with keeping Donn from reentering his home, and keeping everyone above from suffering his wrath. "Have you heard any rumblings about him?"

"Nary a word," he replied. "Is Aodhan here?"

"He's in the apartment. I came down to look for shoes."

Lorcan glanced at my bare feet. "There are sandals and such on the back wall. Give a yell if you need me."

I went toward the display, while Lorcan went behind the counter and started getting the shop ready for the day. He'd been the shop manager longer than Aodhan or I had been alive, and he'd proven his worth many times over. I don't know if we would have been able to defeat Donn without his help.

The sandal display was overwhelming, to say the least. There were men's shoes, women's, kids... water shoes, sandals... And amid this multitude of footwear, there wasn't a single pair of runners like mine. My runners had been ruined while Corentin and godawful Nahel kept me prisoner in a godawful cave beneath the sea, and I couldn't even replace them.

"Bastards," I whispered, as hot tears rolled down my cheeks. "Bloody awful bastards."

"Meri, I can help you find something," Lorcan called, but I ignored him. I'd been kidnapped and humiliated and now my favorite shoes were gone forever.

"Lorcan," Aodhan yelled, as he bounded into the shop. "What's the what, my friend?"

I didn't turn around, but I heard Aodhan and Lorcan speaking to each other in hushed tones. Out of the corner of my eye, I saw Lorcan lock the shop's front door and then disappear into the stockroom. Moments later, I felt Aodhan's hand on my shoulder.

"Mer," he began, then I turned into him and bawled against his chest. I hadn't cried once during this whole ordeal, not when I was so hungry my stomach cramped in on itself, or when Corentin beat me so badly I could hardly move. Instead, I'd been mad, and determined to get away from them and find my way home. Now I was home and safe in Aodhan's arms, and everything came rushing out.

"Let it out, love," Aodhan said, as he held the hysterical mess that was me. "I've got you. Let it out."

"Why am I so upset over shoes?" I mumbled. "Stupid runners aren't even important."

"They're important." Aodhan cupped my face with his hands, and wiped my cheeks with his thumbs. "All of this is important." I nodded, but the tears wouldn't stop flowing.

"We don't have to go to Evonium today," he said. "We don't have to go at all. You've been through enough, Meri. You can stay here, far away from Ker Ys and whatever they've got brewing."

"I can't," I said. "Believe me, I want nothing more than to hide under to covers with you, but I can't. They'll just keep coming after me, and they're after Kevin, too. I want this over with, the sooner the better."

"My brave one." Aodhan pushed back my hair and kissed my forehead. "Just grab a pair of whatever for now. We can stop by your house and get some more supplies for the road, and we'll pick up your other shoes, too."

"We can?" I'd assumed we were leaving straight from the shop.

"Of course we can." Aodhan reached past me to the display shelves, grabbed a pair of tan sandals, and pulled off the tags. "Here. This brand's comfortable."

"How do you know my shoe size?" I asked, as I slipped them on. He was right; the sandals were comfortable, and they fit me perfectly.

"I pay attention," he replied with a wink. "Come on, let's tell Lorcan where we're going. He worries like an old granny when he doesn't know where we are."

We found Lorcan in the farthest corner of the stockroom, pretending to inventory a rack of wet suits. "I should apologize for my outburst," I said, but he shook his head.

"No, you shouldn't," Lorcan said. "I've been dealing with these sorts of occurrences for a long time, now. I know all too well the toll it can take on a body, even a strong one like you."

I looked down at my toes. "I don't feel strong."

"Nonsense. You're here, and you're free, and from what Aodhan says you fought back against your captors and hurt one of them," Lorcan said. "Sounds plenty strong to me."

"Thank you," I said, mostly just to watch Lorcan get all flustered. I would worry about feeling strong later on. "Have you ever heard of a place called Evonium?"

"I have," he replied. "I take it you two are headed that way?"

"We are," Aodhan said. "Meri's aunt has an army up there. Care to join us?"

"I need to stay here and guard what's below, but I'll let Rose and the rest know the plan," Lorcan said. "Around here, many of us are loyal to Kilstiffen. Steinar's a good king, and we'll stand by him."

"I didn't know so many knew of him," I said, now choked up for an entirely different reason.

"Steinar's stood between us and the monsters a time or two. One thing we've all got around here are long memories. If he sends out the call to fight, we'll be there." Lorcan and Aodhan shook hands. "Don't worry, I'll keep the shop safe in your absence."

"I know you will," Aodhan said. "And don't you worry about us, either. We'll be back before you know it."

The drive from the surf shop to my house passed in the blink of an eye. As we pulled up to the place my family had called home for five generations, I was struck by how empty it seemed.

"The house is just lifeless," I said. "It's like no one's been here in years."

"Quite a change from the party last week," Aodhan said, as he parked the car behind the house. "When I came back here without you..."

His voice caught, then he shook his head. "Let's have a look 'round, and pack up some supplies. Want me to get the door for you?"

"I've got it." As I exited the car, my gaze traveled around the property. The remains of the party were still evident, as was an apple tree that had been hacked nearly to bits. I guessed that was the tree Mama had taken her anger out on. When we went inside, the house was in a similar state of disarray.

"They timed this," I said, as I took in the disorganized mess of my kitchen. My family had been so distraught over my disappearance they hadn't even put their used plates in the sink. "They made sure I was taken the day after my parents' renewed their vows, and the day before my birthday. Corentin and Nahel timed this to make sure their plan hurt us as much as possible."

"We made it easy for them, too," Aodhan said. "Everyone knew about the ceremony. Remember all the delegates from the other sea kingdoms? Ker Ys didn't even need to send a spy above to learn what we were up to."

"Corentin has held this grudge against my mother for all these years." I began gathering up the plates and cups, and stacking them on the counter. "When I was below, I taunted him about how my mother rejected him, and the beating Da gave him way back when they met. That's what made him mad enough to hit me."

Aodhan began scraping plates into the bin. "Do you know how many times he hit you?"

"I couldn't have counted if I tried. At least five times. Maybe a dozen. Why?"

"Because that's how many times I am going to hit him." Having finished with the plates, Aodhan grabbed the dish soap. "I'll wash, you dry?"

And so we handled the washing up, and once that was done, we cleaned the rest of the kitchen and set it to rights. It was a small thing to do, but having one corner of my life in order somehow made the rest of the chaos a bit more bearable. What really helped was that Aodhan had known what cleaning the kitchen would mean to me, without me ever saying a word.

"What should we do now?" I asked. Part of me wanted to start straightening up the rest of the house. However, that would just be me wasting time and avoiding going north to join up with my aunt's army. "Pack for the trip?"

"What does one bring to a war against an evil sea kingdom?" Aodhan mused, then he held out his hand. "Come on. I've got a few backpacks up in my room."

We went upstairs to his room, and passed Kevin and Kelsey's door along the way. "Are you certain you want to live above the shop? There's more room here."

"True, but we have our own bathroom and kitchen at the shop," he said. "I've just got the one room here, not like Kevin with his massive apartment across the hall."

"Kevin did all of that work himself." One day, my brother decided to knock down all the interior walls on his side of the second floor, and made himself a three-room suite. "I'm sure he would help you enlarge your side, if you wanted. Or if you wanted to stay at the shop, he could help you install a door at the top of the stairs."

"We do need more privacy, no matter where we end up." Aodhan led me into his room, then he faced me. "Are you thinking up places for just me to live, or for us to live together?"

"Us," I replied, surprised he would even ask that. "Did you think I was trying to get rid of you?"

"We never got to talk on the boat, then everything happened to you, and I..." He ran a hand over his hair. "I didn't want to assume I knew what you wanted."

"I have to tell you something. I was going to tell you on the boat, but I never got the chance." I took his hands, and continued, "You know how you always hear me humming or muttering, but no one else does? And how sometime you think you hear me singing, when I'm not?"

"I do hear you," Aodhan said. "I hear you all the time."

"You are hearing me, but I'm not speaking or singing," I said. "Scáthach told me that a merrow's mate hears their heart, not their voice. Mama confirmed that Da heard her all the way across the bay, and scoured the coast until he found her."

"Wait. You're telling me that your heart is singing to me?"

"What Scáthach said was that a merrow's heart calls to their mate."

Aodhan's face was split by the widest, happiest grin I'd ever seen. "And your heart called to me because you love me?"

"Yeah." I stood on my toes, and wound my arms around his neck. "It's because I love you."

"I've been hearing you mutter and mumble for years," he said as his hands settled on my hips, because of course he couldn't resist a bit of interrogating. "All that time you pretended you didn't like me, and now the truth comes out."

"I always liked you," I said. "I just didn't know what to do about it."

"Good thing we're past all that," he said, then he picked me up under my thighs. I wrapped my legs around his waist, and he carried me to bed. We'd slept there together so many times, always chastely with our clothes on and our hands kept mostly to ourselves. But now we were alone in the house, and if this past week had taught me anything, it was to not waste time with those you love.

"Want to break the no air mattress rule?"

I laughed, and laced my fingers behind his neck. "That rule ends now."

THE ROAD TO ANTRIM

We ended up leaving for County Antrim close to sunset. It was nice having the house to ourselves, and we took our time packing supplies and loading up Aodhan's car. However, we did not dawdle. Many people, including my family, were waiting on us. We went about our work efficiently, but we didn't rush, either.

Once the car was packed up, I made us something to eat, along with a few sandwiches and other snacks for the drive northward. When we'd prepared as much as we could, I locked up the house and we were off.

"Should take us around five hours to get there," Aodhan said, as he checked the route on his phone's GPS. "Which means that when we get there, it'll be dark. Does this attraction close at night?"

"I've no idea." I searched up Giant's Causeway on my own phone, while Aodhan navigated the village streets. "There's a visitor centre. It opens at nine in the morning."

"I hope we don't get banned from this one, like we did at the Cliffs of Moher." Aodhan glanced at me, and barely suppressed a smile as he added, "Try not to jump off anything."

"I'll do my best." I enlarged the map of the area. "I don't think we'll have to deal with the centre, anyway. We can just park elsewhere and walk down to the coast, although it looks like it'll be quite the hike."

"Sounds like what we did when we went up to the Shannon Pot," Aodhan said. "We were lucky we had good weather for that trip. Good thing we packed rain gear this time around," he added, as he shot a look toward rain spattering the windshield.

"Yeah." I scrolled through the legends attached to the Causeway. "Says here the Causeway was created when Fionn mac Cumhaill built a bridge from Ireland to Scotland so he could beat up a giant. I wonder if that's the bridge Mama's sending for us?"

"Could be," Aodhan said. "Either way, won't this be a sight to see."

"Shannon," I mumbled, as I blinked myself awake. Slowly, I remembered that I was in Aodhan's car, and that we were headed north to County Antrim.

"What's that?" Aodhan asked.

"Nothing," I mumbled. "Leftover from a dream, I suppose."

Aodhan moved his hand from the gearshift and set it on my knee. "Did you have a good rest?"

I touched the side window, and let the cool glass help me wake up. "How long was I out?"

"Around two hours. We're about to cross the River Shannon. Is that why you said Shannon just now?"

"I'm not sure," I said, then I realized what he'd said. "We can't cross the river! Mama said to stay on land!"

"I thought she said stay off the sea."

"All the water's connected," I said, then I spied a sign for the up-coming bridge. "Can we pull off, just for a minute? Maybe there's a way around the river."

Aodhan didn't say anything, but he pulled off the main road and found a place to park the car. "We can avoid crossing the river at this spot, but it will add some time to our trip," he said, as he tried out new routes on his GPS. "Although, there's really no way to avoid crossing water entirely. Earlier, while you were sleeping, we crossed the River Fergus, and nothing happened."

I worried my lower lip. "There's got to be a reason why I woke up just now, saying Shannon. Can we go by foot, and get closer to the river? Just to see if anything happens?"

Aodhan leaned forward and looked around. "We can walk down to the water. I see a trail just there." I followed his gaze, and saw a footpath. Suddenly, the water seemed too close, but this had been my idea. Tamping down my unease, I got out of the car and followed Aodhan toward the river's edge. The rain had eased off, which was nice. When we were about two metres from the water, he shot out an arm and blocked my path.

"This is close enough," Aodhan said. "I'm not risking anything reaching out and grabbing you."

"That only happened because the bracelet cut me," I said, though I didn't try to get any nearer to the shore. Aodhan draped his arm across my shoulders, and we contemplated the wide, flat river.

"It's a beautiful night," I murmured. The moon was nearly full, and it reflected on the river's glasslike surface. "I don't know if I've ever seen the river so still. It's like it's not even flowing."

"Can't surf here," Aodhan said, because of course he would assess a river for potential waves—then something rippled near the far shore.

"What's that?" I asked.

"Get behind me," Aodhan said, as he put himself between me and the water. "Mer, I think we should get out of here."

"Wait," I said, then I sang a note to reveal that which was hidden. Before our eyes, the bright white moonlight coalesced into the shape of a woman.

"Shannon," I said, because it must be her. Only, who was she?

"Sionnan, actually," she said. "I felt the pearl nearby, and hoped you would stop to talk."

I clutched my pendant. "You know Manannán?"

"He's my grandfather," Sionnan replied. "You're Meri, are you not?"

"I am." When Sionnan looked at me expectantly, I added, "Forgive me for being a bit standoffish, but almost everyone I've met recently has turned out to be right awful."

Sionnan bowed her head. "I know something of your trials, and I am so very sorry I couldn't come to your aid. I am confined to these waters, and while the river is vast and strong, there are many places I cannot reach."

"You knew I'd been kidnapped?"

"Many of us did," Sionnan replied. "When you called out for help, we of the river heard your cries, but we could not reach you."

"All the stone kept me hidden," I said, and Sionnan nodded. "Is it safe for us to cross the river here?"

"Truth be told, it isn't, but I will do what I can to guard your passage," Sionnan said. "As for your man, I have a gift for him. There is a stone resting upon the shore that can repel any enemy. Find it, and take it on your quest with you."

"All right," Aodhan said, though he sounded rather skeptical. "What does this stone look like?"

"You'll know it when you see it," Sionnan said, then a cloud passed over the moon, and she faded away.

"That was enlightening," I muttered. "I got an apology, and you get a stone."

"I get to look for a stone," Aodhan said, as he withdrew his phone and activated the torch. "Whether or not I find it is a different situation entirely." He approached the water, sweeping the beam of his torch up and down the length of the shore. I did the same, lending my phone's meager light.

"Are you really going to check each and every stone?" I asked.

"How else will I find it?"

"Like this," I replied, then I sang again, and asked the river to reveal the stone Sionnan mentioned. By the time I paused for breath, there was an emerald green glow on the shore a few metres away from us.

"Have I told you how much I love your voice?" Aodhan asked, as he walked toward the glow. I watched him collect the stone, then I noticed the ripples on the far shore. They seemed a bit taller than they had a few moments ago.

"Does the Shannon ever have waves?" I asked.

"Not this far inland," Aodhan replied, then the clouds moved on and the moonlight revealed what was happening out on the water. Despite what Aodhan had said, waves were rolling across the river toward us, and I could see white legs and hooves protruding from the foam.

All at once, I remembered when Donn Dumhach attacked us as the sea bull. I tried to sing a defense, but my voice was shrill and the notes uneven, my terror over facing Donn again making my song discordant.

The waves crashed onto the river's surface, and a line of five white horses emerged from the spray.

"Meri," Aodhan yelled. "Is that Donn?"

"Salt," I said. "We need Key Ys's salt!"

I hated needing something from Ker Ys, but that salt was our only hope. The substance had defeated Donn before, when we faced him at the surf shop, and could do so again. As my song reached for the dregs of the salt I'd left on the beach, a second woman erupted from the water between us and the horses.

"Hold," she commanded, and the water horses halted as one. The woman turned to face me, and I recognized her mahogany hair and striking green eyes instantly.

Dahut.

"Why are you here?" I demanded. "Are those horses Donn's new form?"

Dahut shook her head. "The horses have nothing to do with Donn."

"Did Corentin or Nahel send you?"

"No," she said. "I've left Ker Ys, and I'm on your side. I don't agree—"

"You expect me to believe that?" I took a step toward her. "You see this?" I demanded, pointing toward my bruised, scabbed face. "Your uncle beat me bloody. Your filthy brother told me—in excruciating, graphic detail—what he would do to me!"

"Nahel—"

"Nahel is a perverse beast," I shrieked. "Do you know what they did to me? What they planned to do to me, and my brother? I can hardly sleep. Every time I close my eyes, I either see Corentin looming over me about to strike, or Nahel leering at me, waiting to get his hands on me."

I paused for breath, panting and furious and how dare she come near me after what her family had done to mine? Aodhan took his place next to me, his arms crossed over his chest and magic stone in hand.

"Well?" Aodhan asked. "Meri asked you why you're here. Answer, or leave."

"I've already left everything I've ever known behind," Dahut said. "I haven't agreed with my father's policies for some time, but when they created those bracelets to ensnare you and your brother, they went too far."

"Such altruism, especially from one who hardly knows me," I said.

"It wasn't just that they wanted to abduct you both, and force you to comply with them," Dahut continued. "Those bracelets used up the last of our gold. Our people are starving, and instead of using what was left of our wealth to feed them, they sought power and revenge like the fools they are."

"If you were against all of this, why didn't you warn us?" I asked. "You know exactly where we live."

"By the time I learned what they were going to do, the delegate was already on its way to deliver the bracelets to you and Kevin," Dahut replied. "I was too late."

"But you could have told us where they were holding Meri," Aodhan said. "They had her for six days. You could have come to any of us, and helped us rescue her."

"No, I couldn't have," she replied. "Aoife would have killed me on site, for one. For two, the prison caves are warded. Corentin would have known the moment I set foot below."

"Six days," Aodhan seethed. "Can you imagine what it's like being held captive for six days?"

Dahut met his gaze. "Believe me, I know how much my uncle can hurt someone in six days."

The waver in her voice made me believe her, but it didn't make me trust her. "What about those horses?" I asked, nodding toward the line of perfectly still equines hovering above the river's surface. "They look suspiciously like the ones on Ker Ys's standard. And they just happened to be following me?"

"They're called the Camargue," Dahut replied. "They live in the shallows near Ker Ys. Corentin sent them after you, but they don't like him. If I tell them to leave you be, they will."

"Oh, so you're the water horse whisperer now?" I asked. "The wave dancer with a heart of gold? What's your game, Dahut?"

"I want to join Kilstiffen against Ker Ys," she said. "The council and Ker Ys want to take over Kilstiffen, but that's only the beginning." She took a step toward me. "You dealt with my brother and uncle for six days, but I've been dealing with them for my entire life. No one knows how much they need to be stopped more than me."

"What about Gradlon?" I asked.

Dahut swallowed hard, and looked away. "Corentin killed him."

Stunned, I glanced at Aodhan. His mouth was a slash across his face, and a muscle twitched in his jaw.

"I'm sorry for your loss," I said. "And I believe you wish to leave Ker Ys behind. However, I also don't want you coming with me." I sang toward the water, which churned with the riverbed and thickened to a heavy sludge around Dahut's feet and the water horses' hooves.

"What are you doing?" Dahut demanded.

"I can't have you following us," I replied. "I'm not sure how long you'll be stuck like this, but if I hit the proper notes the water will revert to normal at sunrise. Then you can go on to Kilstiffen and plead your case to the king. Whatever happens afterward will be up to him."

Dahut nodded. "And if I don't go to Steinar?"

"Go, don't go, it's up to you." I turned off the torch on my phone and pocketed it. Aodhan did the same, and we began the return trip up the path. "It's your life. Do what you like with it."

"Meri," Dahut called. "I'm not like Nahel!"

"Prove it," I called back.

We returned to the car. Wordlessly, Aodhan started it, then we resumed our trip and drove across the bridge. As we passed over the water, I saw Dahut and the water horses watching us from the mud pit I'd trapped them in.

"Do you really see them whenever you close your eyes?" Aodhan asked, once we'd cleared the river.

"Yes," I replied. "Corentin hurt me so badly, but what Nahel said..." I shuddered, and hunched down in my seat. "He never touched me, but somehow those words hurt just as much."

Aodhan reached over, and took my hand. "We're going to make them pay. I don't know what sort of a justice system Kilstiffen or the council has, but Corentin and Nahel are going to be held accountable for every single hurt you suffered, physical or otherwise. I'll make certain of it." He squeezed my fingers, and added, "And if those nightmares come back, just roll over and wake me up. I'll help you forget them."

"You're going to protect me from my dreams?"

"Your heart called to me," he said. "It's now my job to keep it safe, awake or asleep."

GIANT'S CAUSEWAY

After our run-in with Dahut and her herd of water horses, I stayed awake for the rest of the drive to County Antrim. Being that our foes were now appearing out of the water, salt and otherwise, I didn't want to risk us being attacked while I was asleep. I spent the time researching the Giant's Causeway on my phone, handing Aodhan sandwich after sandwich, and examining the stone Sionnan had given him.

"Other than the color, it's quite unremarkable." The stone was smooth and heavy, like river rock, and fit neatly in the palm of my hand. It was also an amazingly bright green. "Do you think the colour is what makes it magical?"

"No idea, Mer," Aodhan said. "Sionnan said it would repel any foe. Maybe we need to be around the bad guys for it to activate?"

"But how does it know," I murmured, as I held the stone close to my face. "Do we tell it who's evil, or does it somehow sense evil intent?"

"I bet your ma or aunt will know. Or maybe Evonium has a wizard academy with some books on magic stones. Fancy a bit of research?"

I glanced at him, unsure if he was joking. "Before Scáthach went home, did she tell you anything about her academy?"

"Oh, yes. She told me that she's been training classes of warriors up there for years," Aodhan replied.

"I wonder why she's training warriors in Evonium instead of in Kilstiffen," I mused.

"Steinar couldn't keep such a large force in Kilstiffen without the council asking a bunch of questions," Aodhan said. "So Scáthach went north to find a suitable place for a second force, should the need for one arise, they pretended to banish Oscar down to Tir na nÓg so he could act as a spy, and Aoife stayed home to protect the city."

I almost asked Aodhan how he'd learned all of this, but it was obvious that my mother and aunt had shared quite a lot of information with him while I was gone. "We've been wary of Ker Ys for some time, then," I said.

"Apparently it all came to a head when your ma refused Corentin, but then MacCreehy and his plan to permanently raise Kilstiffen threw a wrench in everything," he replied. "Even with that setback, everyone kept at it. Oscar gathered a great deal of information, and Scáthach's army just kept growing. The academy's got five thousand full-fledged soldiers, and more still in training."

"That's amazing." When Scáthach had mentioned her training academy, I'd imagined a small establishment, not a full military operation. "Do we know how many soldiers Ker Ys has? Although Dahut said their people are starving."

"Smart rulers always feed the army first," Aodhan said. "But it's not just Ker Ys we need to worry about. The real villain is the council, and whichever kingdoms they've gotten on their side."

"What is the council's problem?" I wondered aloud. I hadn't expected Aodhan to know the answer to that as well, but he replied right away.

"According to your ma, the council is a leftover from a rather large kingdom that sank some time ago, but unlike when Kilstiffen went down, that place was destroyed," Aodhan replied. "Apparently, a volcano erupted, and the ensuing disaster was too much for the kingdom to recover from. But this city was by far the biggest and most powerful of them all, and the remaining administrators formed the council we know and despise today."

"How could one city that no longer exists still hold such sway over the rest?" I asked. "Do you know what this place was called?"

"Get this. Atlantis!"

"No way," I said, awed that such a place had been real. Then again, I regularly went down to Kilstiffen, which was one floor above the land of the gods, and I wore a necklace that I could use on to call the god of the sea. "Of all things to be real. But it must have gone down centuries ago. How is the council still around?"

"You're right, it did sink a while ago, but apparently it held influence over most of the known world," Aodhan replied. "And Atlantis was huge. It stretched from where the Atlantic meets the Mediterranean all the way toward North America. After the eruption, the ruling party evacuated to several other cities and such, and soon afterward they formed a network among themselves. The Atlanteans kept in contact while simultaneously increasing their influence over the remaining kingdoms, and here we are today."

"Here we are, indeed." I gazed at the green stone in my hand, wondering if it, too, had come from Atlantis. Perhaps that would explain its bright hue, and magical properties. "But why are they after Kilstiffen?"

"The short answer? Money. Kilstiffen is the richest of the sea king-doms, and the council wants to make it into a new Atlantis. As you could guess, Steinar's not having it."

"Why does he even put up with them?"

"Tradition?" Aodhan suggested. "Remember, love, this has all been going on since long before he was king."

I moved so I was leaning sideways in my seat, and watched Aod-han's profile. "I like it when you call me love."

"Yeah?" He found my hand and grasped it, and rubbed his thumb across my knuckles. "I like calling you that."

"I need a pet name for you." I'd only ever called him Aodhan. "What are male surfers called?"

"Surfers," he replied. "My dad doesn't have a nickname, either. My ma only ever calls him Lucas."

"Maybe it's a family thing, and Sullivan men are only to be referred to by their given names."

"That could be. Also, looks like we're here."

Aodhan's phone announced that we had reached the end of our route. After cruising past the visitor centre, and verifying that it was indeed closed and the car park thus inaccessible, we looked for a place to stop somewhat close to the shore. Places that were both safe and free to park in overnight were in short supply, but we ended up leaving the car at the railway station.

"From here it should be about three, maybe four kilometers to the Causeway," Aodhan said, as we put on our rain jackets and strapped on our packs. A light drizzle had started up, and I hoped it wouldn't become a downpour like we'd experienced back home. "You sure you're up for the walk? We can always wait for the visitor centre to open up in the morning and grab a shuttle."

"I'll be all right," I said, with more confidence than I felt. My feet were still sore from my trek out of the caves with Oscar, and my legs and back positively ached, but I wanted to keep moving. "Besides, if a bridge from here to Scotland pops out of the water, best it happens at night when there aren't a gaggle of tourists watching."

"Good point." Aodhan closed and locked the rear door of his car, and pocketed the keys. "Let me know when you need to take a break. We don't need to plow straight through."

I bit back my smart comeback; I didn't like being coddled, but Aodhan was only looking out for me. "What did you do while I was... While I was gone? Surely you weren't waiting in that cave the whole time."

"The first thing I did was call Kevin from the boat, and tell him everything that happened," he began. "By the time I got back to your house, your ma and Scáthach had already sent a bunch of messages to Oscar."

"How did they contact Oscar?" I asked, since Oscar hadn't had a phone on him.

"They sang to him, and his reply came around midnight." He glanced at me. "That was a very long time for us to wait."

I took his hand. He squeezed my fingers, then he pulled me toward him and crushed me against his chest. "No one knew if you were alive or... We were fairly certain the council was behind everything, and Aoife said they had to keep you alive for us to meet their demands. Over and over, she kept saying you had to be alive."

"I wish I'd paid attention to you, and never put that bracelet on." Cold drizzle was sluicing down the back of my neck, but I ignored it. Aodhan needed to hold me just as much as I needed to hold him. "I'm sorry I didn't listen."

"You didn't do anything wrong, love." Aodhan gave me a final squeeze, then we resumed walking, though we kept hold of each other's hands. "When your ma got Oscar's message—"

"How did she get it? Was it a scroll?" I asked; I'd seen the gold-capped scrolls sent by Kilstiffen's messengers before.

"His reply was a song. Somehow, Aoife caught it in the air, then her and Scáthach sat down at the kitchen table and analyzed it."

"How on earth did they do that?"

"They sang it to each other, back and forth like birds."

An image of my mother and aunt chirping at each other flitted behind my eyes. "I had no idea that was even possible."

"Nor did I. But decipher it they did, and they figured out that Oscar would bring you into that stalactite chamber in Tallulah's cave in about three days' time. Then Scáthach announced she would return to Evonium to rally the troops, and there was some more discussion about who should go where."

"And out of all the places you could have gone, you picked the cave?"

"Of course I did," he replied, then I remembered something else he'd said.

"You thought I would be there in three days, but it took me six days to get there. Even though I was late, you kept on waiting for me."

"Yeah. I did." He glanced at me. "Those last few days were hard, but I couldn't give up. Your family believed in Oscar, so I had to believe in him, too. I had to believe that he would bring you back to me. That belief... It was all I had."

I pressed myself against his side, remembering how my belief that Aodhan would look for me kept me going while I was a prisoner. "I'll always come back to you."

The walk from the railway station to the Causeway took us around an hour. The drizzle kept up, and by the time the field of basalt hexagons came into view, I was a soaked, shivering mess. However, neither my miserable state nor the dark and rainy night detracted from the amazing sight before us. The coastline was covered in geometric stone columns that began on the cliffs, and extended all the way down to the shore and under the sea.

"There's supposed to be thousands of these columns," Aodhan said. "I wonder who counted them all?"

"Let's not add maths to this adventure." A maths-induced headache was the last thing I needed. "Where do you think the bridge will appear?"

Aodhan paused, and looked around the area. "No idea. Let's get to a high point, and see if anything looks bridgelike."

I nodded, and followed him as he climbed ever higher up the columns. The drizzle had made everything slippery, and it wasn't long before I lost my footing and landed hard on my knee.

"Meri," Aodhan called, then he was at my side. "Are you all right?"

"Fine," I grumbled, even though I'd skinned my already injured knee. "Let's keep going."

"Maybe we should rest," he said. Ignoring him, I tried to get to my feet. My knee had other ideas, and I went down on my bottom.

"All right," I said. "We can rest a bit, but only until I can get up."

Aodhan sat down next to me, and draped his arm across my back. "Maybe we don't find the bridge, and it finds us. Can you sing a message to your ma, like she did to Oscar?"

"I suppose I can," I said, though I had no idea how to do that, then I spied something in the distance. It was a rock outcropping, which wasn't at all unusual at the Causeway. However, instead of an angular basalt column, this feature was all undulating curves.

"Are there statues here?" I asked. Aodhan followed my gaze, then he stood to get a better look at the statue. After a moment, he laughed.

"Meri, I know how we'll find the way," he said, as he helped me to my feet. My knee wasn't happy about being upright, but I managed. I leaned heavily on Aodhan as I hobbled toward the statue, and was gobsmacked when I recognized her. And yes, this statue was definitely a her.

"Tallulah," I cried, as I threw my arms around the stone merrow's neck. Her skin was smooth and cool, like the living rock she was made of. "I'm so glad to see you!"

"I'm glad to be seen, Meri girl," she said, as she patted my back. "Hello, Aodhan. Still following this one around?"

"To the ends of the earth," he replied. "How have you been?"

"Better than you two, I'm afraid," Tallulah replied. "I've heard that you've had a rough go of late?"

"That is an understatement," I said, as I drew back. Tallulah looked just the same as when we'd met her down in the caves that led to Kilstiffen, though at the time she'd told us she was called Tourmaline, Jewel of the Sea. "The stalactite in the cave where we met you? I sort of wrecked it."

"Oscar told me all about the fight, and the fact that you made the great stalactite fall onto your foes means that you did the right thing," she said. "I assume you're here so I can summon the bridge, and then you two will hop over to Evonium?"

"Yes, please."

"All right, then. Stand back."

Tallulah slithered down onto her stomach, and set her hands flat on the columns. The sound of rock grinding against rock rumbled up from the coast. As I watched, dozens and then hundreds of columns rose from the sea. One by one, the columns fused together, forming a bridge that stretched across the ocean farther than my eyes could see. When the floor was complete, walls grew up and out of the bottom level and met each other above the walkway to form a roof. Lastly, arched windows set themselves into the walls at regular intervals.

"That is the true Giant's Causeway," Tallulah said, as she sat up and tossed her hair over her striated limestone shoulder. "Follow it, and it will lead you straight to The Shadow's door."

"Thank you, Tallulah," I said. "Yet again, you've come through for us when we needed you most."

"Think nothing of it," she said. "But I would ask that whenever you see a field of stone such as this, you will remember me."

"We will," I promised, then Aodhan and I stepped onto the Causeway to begin the last leg of our trek to Evonium. We had an army to meet.

A SMALL REUNION

Walking from Northern Ireland to Scotland took a long time. Even Aodhan's legendary stamina couldn't handle the distance, and we ended up taking a short rest about an hour after we got on the bridge. That rest turned out to not nearly be enough, and it wasn't long before I was reluctantly asking for another break.

"All right," Aodhan said, as he swept his gaze up and down the bridge. We hadn't seen or heard anyone else, but Dahut and her herd of water horses were still out there galloping across the waves, not to mention the rest of our enemies. "Let's set up here for a few minutes."

He chose a spot between two of the windows, and set our packs against the wall; he'd picked mine up after our last break, and I hadn't complained once about him carrying it. As soon as the packs were on the ground, I sat down and laid my head against one as if it was a pillow, and the world faded to black.

"Meri."

I sat straight up, and pulled the covers up to my neck. I was in my opulent bedroom in Kilstiffen's palace, and whomever had just called out my name wasn't Aodhan.

"Meri. Are you ready for me?"

"Stay away!" I yelled. "Don't come in here!"

"But you're my wife now," Nahel said, as he stepped into view. "Where else would I sleep, but with you?"

I screamed, both in my dream and with my physical voice. Aodhan jolted awake, then he scooped me into his arms.

"I've got you," he said, as I shivered and clutched his shirt. "I'm here."

"The dreams are getting more realistic," I said; while I'd been having them regularly since my escape, this was the first time I'd woken up screaming. "Do you think they laid an enchantment on me?"

"If they did, we're getting it off," Aodhan began, then he paused.

"What is it?"

"Someone's coming." He released me, and stood. I could hear rapid footsteps against the stone; whoever was approaching us was running as if their life depended on it.

"Should we hide?" I asked, not that there was any place for us to go. Just as I was about to try and replicate Oscar's obfuscation glamour, Aodhan pulled me to my feet.

"Meri, look," Aodhan said. I looked down the causeway, and saw a woman running toward us. For a moment I thought she was some sort of bridge guard sent to apprehend us, then she passed a window and I saw the starlight reflect off her gold chain mail.

"Mama," I called, as I took a step toward her. I'd barely managed that before she reached us, and I was wrapped up in her arms.

"Meri, my Meri girl," Mama said, as she cradled me against her. "I'm so glad you're here. I'm so glad you're safe."

"How did you know we would be here?" I asked.

"I saw the bridge rise up to meet you, and your father and I have been waiting at our end ever since," she replied. "When I heard you scream, I ran." She drew back, and held my face in her hands. Her brows pinched as she took in my bruises, and the multitude of cuts and scrapes on my cheek and forehead. "Gods below, Meri, what happened to you?"

"Corentin," I replied. "He's insane."

My mother nodded. "He is, and he'll pay for this." She turned to Aodhan. "Give me your packs. I'll carry them for you. You kept to land on the way north?"

"We avoided the sea," Aodhan replied as he handed over our packs. "Crossed a few rivers, and those were mostly quiet."

"Mostly?" Mama asked.

"At The Shannon, we met Sionnan," I replied. "She gave Aodhan a stone." Aodhan showed my mother the bright green stone that had been sitting on the river's shore.

"We also ran into Dahut, and a group of water horses," Aodhan said.

"That must have been quite the encounter," Mama said, as we began walking. "The Camargue are blood bonded to Ker Ys's royal family. Did Gradlon send them after you?"

"Dahut told us that Gradlon is dead," I replied. "Corentin murdered him."

My mother nodded. "That complicates things, but it will strengthen our position against Ker Ys. How did you leave things with Dahut?"

"Meri trapped them in mud so they couldn't follow us," Aodhan said.

"Ah. Didn't believe her story, then?" Mama asked.

"She said she wanted to join us," I began, then I spied another figure up ahead. My father was standing at the end of the bridge.

"Da," I called, then I used up my last bit of energy as I ran to him.

"I can't run as fast as your mother," he began, then I threw myself into his arms. I loved my mother, but something about Da's strong arms and scratchy wool jumpers was always home for me. "Missed you, Meri girl."

"Missed you too, Da." I drew back, and saw Da's wet cheeks.

"Why'd you yell just now?" he asked.

"I fell asleep back there, had a bit of a nightmare," I replied. "Ker Ys has addled my brain."

"You and me both," he said, then he embraced me again. "Tell me what you need, and it's yours."

"Is Kevin here?" I asked, and Da replied that he was. "I'm fine, then. I just need to know that everyone I love is safe."

"Aye, Meri girl, you and I want the same." Da smoothed my hair away from my face. "We've got almost the whole family together. Steinar's still below, but we'll meet up with him soon."

"And Niamh?" I asked.

"Niamh went to her father to rally reinforcements," Da replied.

"So it really is a war."

"We've been on the brink of one for years," Mama said, as she and Aodhan joined us. "My betrothal to Corentin was a last ditch effort to keep the peace. Your and Kevin's existence proves how futile that was."

"Good thing you'd already met Mr Murphy before that lout came along," Aodhan said.

"Actually, I was betrothed to Corentin the day before I met Brian," Mama said, then she laced her fingers with Da's. "And even if I'd never met my beloved man, there was no way I would ever marry Corentin."

"Why didn't a war begin right after you refused him?" I asked, since waiting twenty-odd years seemed like a ridiculously long time to hold a grudge, and enact your revenge.

"Well, that was also my fault," Mama replied. "After I stole the key to the city, and Kilstiffen was trapped below the sea, Gradlon decided we weren't worth the bother. However, even though Kilstiffen remained below, we continued to prosper while Ker Ys's fortunes dwindled. Gradlon's empty treasury made him increasingly desperate, and it's easy for a desperate man to be swayed."

"Which is how the council got their hooks into him," I concluded. "They really want to recreate that long gone Atlantis on Kilstiffen?"

"Aye, and what a foolish plan it is," Mama said, then we reached the end of the causeway. "We'll talk more about it after you've had a rest, and a look around. Welcome to Evonium!"

WELCOME TO EVONIUM

The first and most obvious fact I learned about Evonium was that it was above ground.

I'd expected it to be a sea kingdom like Kilstiffen, and therefore beneath the water. However, I'd also never been to any of the other kingdoms, so for all I knew, the rest of them were set above the waves and Kilstiffen was the outlier. Regardless, the island that housed the city of Evonium stretched out along the western coast of Scotland like a cat relaxing in a sunbeam.

"It reminds me of the Roman Empire," Aodhan said. We had just exited the Causeway, and from our vantage point, we could see much of the city. Everything from the many towers to the roads consisted of precise stone blocks. I couldn't wait to see it in the daylight.

"All these bridges and roads look like they were built by centurions," he continued.

"Some of them were," Scáthach said, as she joined us. "A Roman legion went north into Scotland around two thousand years ago. They got lost for a bit before they found a new mission, and built the foundations of what you see today. Meri, let me look at you."

I turned toward my aunt, and held myself still as she scrutinized every visible mark and blemish upon my skin. Finally, she nodded.

"You look like a warrior who fought well, and won," she said. I let out a relieved breath; I hadn't realized how much her approval would mean to me. "Now, vengeance is ours to be had."

"Must it be about revenge?" I asked. "Ker Ys has been fueled by vengeance for all these years, and it's nearly destroyed them. I'd rather have a good, honest victory."

Scáthach bowed her head. "You're wise, I'll give you that. And yes, any warrior worth their salt will always take a clean victory over revenge. However, you are the heiress to the city, and you were targeted as a way to make all of Kilstiffen suffer. Therefore, we must reciprocate in kind."

I nodded; I didn't like all this talk about war and revenge, but I understood Scáthach's position. "And Evonium will reciprocate, as well?"

"We will, as will several other sea kingdoms," Scáthach said. "Since word has gotten out of your abduction, Gradlon's allies are turning away from him."

"Gradlon's dead," I said.

Scáthach's mouth was a grim line. "Do you know when he died?"

"No, but according to his daughter, Corentin killed him."

"Do you believe her?"

"I'm not sure," I admitted. "I believe that Gradlon's dead, but I'm not certain I understand why she told me."

"Could have been a bag of lies," Aodhan said. "She wanted to come here with us. Said she was defecting from Ker Ys and wanted to join up with Kilstiffen."

"What did you say to that?" Scáthach asked.

"I didn't say much," I replied. "I did trap her and her water horses so they couldn't follow us to the Causeway."

"You trapped the Camargue?" Scáthach asked, as her eyebrows shot halfway up her head. When I nodded, she glanced at Mama. "Meri, for all that you began using your voice later on, it hasn't dampened your strength in the slightest. The Camargue are powerful, Dahut more so."

I shrugged. "I didn't feel powerful at the time. I just wanted them to leave me and Aodhan alone."

"And you succeeded," Scáthach said. "Come. I'll show you where you can rest."

We followed Scáthach down a wide staircase and into Evonium's streets. As Aodhan asked my aunt questions about the academy, I hung back with my mother.

"Oscar told me you were held in the same caves where they kept me," I said without preamble. "He told me it took him a long time to find you."

"Aye, it took a very long time," she said. "I was there for so long I'd lost all sense of how long I'd been down there. I'd nearly lost myself completely."

"How did he know where to look for you?"

"He didn't. That's why it took so long to find me." We walked in silence for a moment, with Da a few paces behind us. "I'd been gone for seven years, and as agreed, I was about to reunite with Brian. With you." Mama sighed. "I was so excited to see all of you, to see how you and Kevin had grown... I don't know how Seamus found me. My excitement must have made me careless, caused me to leave clues I would have otherwise left hidden. As soon as I set foot above on the day I was to meet Brian, I was captured."

Mama paused and glanced at Da, then she said, "I've never told anyone what my imprisonment was like."

"You can tell me, if you want," I said. "Or don't. Sometimes, leaving an experience behind is the best thing we can do."

She smiled a bit, and it almost reached her eyes. "Wise words, my lamb. Regardless, my last act before they hauled me below was to scream out a message to my sister. As soon as she received it, she sent Oscar after me, and thirteen months later, he found me."

"Waiting for so long must have been agony," I said. "Did Grandfather know what had happened to you?"

"He did, but as he's the king he needs to move in official circles. I was a criminal at the time." She laughed through her nose. "Perhaps I still am."

"What happened after Oscar found you?"

"He brought me here," Mama replied, encompassing the city with a sweep of her arm. "I was a mess, and it took Scáthach and her healers nearly another thirteen months to restore me to health."

"But they did," I said. "Even though Seamus and the council tried to destroy you, you escaped, and you're still Kilstiffen's greatest warrior."

"Aye, that I am. Perhaps one day, I will pass that title on to you."

"I don't know about that," I said. "Aodhan can be the next warrior. I'll cheer him on from the sidelines."

"Never doubt that warriors' blood runs in your veins, Meri," Mama said. "We're all of us fighters, though we all go about it in different ways."

"Like how Scáthach is a teacher, and you're more of a front line fighter," I said, as my mother nodded. "And Oscar... What sort of fighter is he?"

"No one knows what Oscar does, save for Oscar," Mama said. "Believe me, it's for the best."

"What about Grandfather?" I assumed that someone called Steinar the Immoveable must be formidable in battle. "He's also a warrior, yes?"

"He is, and he'll lead the charge against Ker Ys," Mama said, pride evident in her voice. "As the king, it is his duty and his privilege to be the first in any advance, and the last in every retreat."

"That doesn't sound very safe."

"War never is, my lamb," Mama said, then she indicated a white marble tower that loomed over us at the end of the street. "We're here."

"And where is here?" I asked, as I looked up at the tower. Based on the rows of windows, it had four stories, and a staircase that wrapped around the exterior like a crenellated snake. The roof was covered in trees, and being that the sun was just rising, I saw brightly colored birds, flitting between the branches as they sang hello to the dawn. "Is that tower an aviary of sorts?"

"No, but the songbirds do tend to congregate here. This tower is our family's home here in Evonium. An apartment has already been prepared for you and Aodhan."

"Oh." I stared up at the pristine white and grey edifice as I clasped and unclasped my hands. "You and Da are all right with Aodhan and me staying in the same room?"

"Meri." Mama stopped walking, and set her hands on my shoulders. "I was almost your exact age when my heart first called to Brian. I understand."

"Yes, I suppose you do." I met her eyes, then focused on her feet. "He wants us to get married."

"What do you want?" When I stayed quiet, she said, "Surely you said something after he asked you."

"I... um." I blew out a breath, and hazarded a glance at her face. She looked concerned, and not at all judgmental. "I told him we're too young."

At that, Mama laughed. "You are young, that's true, and you're also very, very practical. Perhaps you should consider being a little less practical, at least where Aodhan's concerned."

"Did you just suggest that your barely eighteen-year-old daughter should marry her first boyfriend?" I demanded, loudly enough for Aodhan, Scáthach, and Da, all of whom were now standing at the tower's entrance, to look over at us.

"I didn't suggest you do anything," she replied with a shrug. "However, no matter how good our brains are at pointing us in the right direction, sometimes we need to let our hearts lead the way."

"Our hearts," I murmured, as I watched Aodhan gesturing wildly as he talked to Da and Scáthach. "How did Da ask you?"

"Ah, well." Mama looped her arm with mine, and we resumed walking. "I'd been above with your father for four entire, wonderful months, but then something happened, and I needed to return to Kilstiffen. He asked me right before I went below."

"What I said was," Da added, as he approached us, with Scáthach and Aodhan close behind, "'when you return, marry me'."

"And I said yes," Mama said, but Da shook his head.

"If I recall, your exact words were, 'when I return, I will marry you, Brian Murphy'." Da took her hand and kissed it. "And you did."

"But you never asked her," I said. "That's not fair, Da. You're supposed to ask."

Da gave me a bemused face, then he said, "Aoife, my beauty, will you marry me a third time?"

"Brian, mo ghra, I will marry you a thousand times," Mama replied.

Scáthach rolled her eyes. "You're both insufferable. Meri, Aodhan, follow me."

Aodhan extended his hand toward me. I clasped it, and we followed Scáthach into the tower.

"You told your ma we're getting married?" Aodhan asked.

"I told her you brought it up, and that I said we're too young," I replied. "She thinks I'm being too practical."

"If there's anything Aoife never was, it's practical," Scáthach said, then she opened a door. "You've been assigned to this half of the second floor. Your brother and Kelsey are in the apartment across the way. And Meri, someone's been waiting for you."

"Who would be waiting for me here," I wondered, then I stepped past my aunt and saw Talia standing in the center of the room.

"I can't believe you're here," I said, as I threw myself into her arms. "Why aren't you in Kilstiffen?"

"Because I'm needed here," she replied. "Remember, the royal children are my charges, and that charge now extends you and Kevin." She drew back and lightly touched my bruised cheek, then she said, "That includes you, too, Aodhan."

"I'm honored, Talia," Aodhan said. "Truly. I assume we have you to thank for this beautiful room?"

"Not only me," Talia replied, as I swept my gaze around the apartment. The floorplan appeared similar to my apartment in Kilstiffen.

We were standing in an atrium, with a lovely black and white marble floor, and was lined with wall niches that contained glass vases filled with fresh flowers. Beyond the arched doorway was a sitting room complete with cushioned benches and arched windows that perfectly matched the door, and filled the room with sunlight. I could see another door at the far end of the room, and assumed it led to a bedroom.

"Now, Meri," Talia said, snapping me out of my reverie, "I know you've had quite the journey to get here, so I do recommend you get some sleep. I've had a light meal laid out for you, and we'll have a formal breakfast with the entire family in a few hours."

"About sleep," I began. "I've been having dreams. Bad ones."

"Hmm," Talia said, as she tapped her chin. "I believe I know of something that will help. Follow me."

Talia led us into the sitting room; out of the corner of my eye, I saw my mother deposit our packs in the atrium, and ease the door shut as she let herself out. I'd wanted to talk to her a bit more, but I assumed she had tasks to attend to before breakfast. At least we would see each other again soon. Of course, Talia's "light meal" was so extensive, I didn't think I'd be hungry at breakfast.

"Look at all this," Aodhan said, as he took in the veritable buffet waiting for us in the sitting room. There were breads and pastries, bowls of fruit, and steaming pots of tea. "I don't know what to start with."

"Try the mixed berry pastry," Talia suggested, then she presented me with a cup of tea. "This should help you sleep."

I accepted the cup, and sniffed the steam. "Chamomile?"

"It's the best way I know of to get a good, restful sleep." Talia smoothed back my hair, then she glided her fingertips over the embroidery she'd done on the shoulder of my sweatshirt. "It seems I only get to visit with you after you've suffered some sort of injury."

"We'll have to fix that," I said; I appreciated Talia so much, and I understood why the royal children had been entrusted to this sweet, kind woman. "I promise I'll visit more, and for good reasons, like to bring you a cake."

"Yes, let's have lots of cakes," Aodhan chimed in.

"That sounds lovely," Talia said. "Now, I'll grant you two a bit of privacy. Get some rest, and I'll return to collect you for breakfast."

We murmured our thanks, and Talia let herself out. Aodhan investigated the breakfast table while I sat on one of the benches and sipped my tea. Aodhan filled a plate with his usual mound of food, then he sat beside me.

"Even I've never had fruit for breakfast," Aodhan said, as he picked up a spray of red berries. "Unless it was something like a banana."

"Sad there's no eggs or sausage?" I asked, since sausage rolls were his favorite. I opened my mouth to speak further, and yawned instead.

"Let's move into the bedroom." Aodhan stood and held out a hand, then he pulled me up and we entered the bedroom. The room was decorated in pristine white with accents of pale blue and green, perhaps to honor Kilstiffen's home under the sea. In the centre of the room was an enormous round bed covered in so many creamy white blankets and pillows it resembled an iceberg. I may have only felt this way due to my profound exhaustion, but it was the most beautiful bed I had ever seen.

"I'll be here." I set my tea on the bedside table, pulled off my boots, and got under the blankets. Heaven. "If anyone comes looking for me, tell them I'm busy."

"Don't you want to get undressed?" Aodhan asked. "Sleeping in jeans won't be comfortable."

"This is fine," I mumbled, then sleep took me.

ALL THE SEA KINGDOMS

I was dreaming again. Being self-aware in a dream is quite an odd feeling and not something I recommend.

Regardless, I was walking through a dark, chilly castle. I could hear waves pounding against the city walls, and assumed I was in Evonium. But even though I'd first seen Evonium in the predawn twilight, it hadn't seemed dark or foreboding, not like this endless shadowy hall that led who knows where. And where were the people? I couldn't see or hear another living soul, and the only sound was that of my footsteps as I walked on.

And on.

Eventually, the hall led me to a large, dark throne room. The front of the room was as devoid of life as the hall was, but I did see something at the far end. Something tall, and angular. The throne, perhaps? I crossed the room, which was easily as big as a football pitch. When I was close enough to make out the throne's details, I was hit with the sharp scent of copper.

No, not copper. Blood.

Dreaming me has always been fearless, so I went around to the front of the throne. Seated atop a dais built like an abattoir was Dahut, wearing a regal red cape around her neck, and a crown of bloody bones set atop her head. Beneath her feet, I could make out Corentin, Nahel, and Gradlon's lifeless faces.

"What happened?" I demanded. "How did they die?"

"Don't you know, Meri?" Dahut asked, as she turned her emerald green gaze toward me. "It's all because of you. Now, you'll help me with the rest, won't you?"

My eyes snapped open, and I took a few deep, cleansing breaths as I stared at the ceiling. *Dahut is not here*, I repeated in my mind. *I am safe in Evonium.* Beside me, Aodhan let out a truly impressive snore, thus reinforcing that I was among family, and no one from Ker Ys could reach me.

Along with feeling safe, I was also hot. I slipped out of bed and pulled off my sweatshirt and jeans, then I visited what served as a bathroom. That accomplished, I got back in bed and curled up against Aodhan's back. My movements disturbed him, and he rolled over and slid an arm around my waist.

"Everything alright?" he mumbled into my hair.

"I had a dream." I moved so we were facing each other. "It wasn't scary, but it was weird."

"Weird how? Like, putting peanut butter in coffee weird, or aliens weird?"

"Somewhere in between. I saw Dahut sitting on a throne of corpses."

"Definitely aliens weird. Did you recognize the corpses?"

"Yeah. They were all her family, then she asked for my help."

Aodhan's eyes snapped open. "Mer, that can't be good. What if that dream was a premonition?"

"Doubtful," I replied. "I've never had a premonition before. And since Gradlon's gone, if Corentin and Nahel are defeated and sent away to prison or wherever, won't Dahut be the next in charge?"

"I guess, but if Corentin and Nahel are sent away, they'll be prisoners, not corpses," he pointed out.

He was right, of course, and a sinking feeling developed in my belly. "What should we do?"

"For now, we should be alert, and cautious," Aodhan replied. "Best case scenario, it really was only a dream."

"And worst case?"

"Worst case, we'll all be very glad you trapped Dahut in the mud back at the Shannon."

Even though Talia had said she'd be by to collect us for breakfast, after I told Aodhan about my bloody dreams. neither of us could sleep any longer. The sun had risen, so we went out to explore Evonium. It really did look like an illustration of Rome in the empire's heyday come to life, what with its buildings faced with columns and topped with peaked roofs, and the wide and flat paved roads that separated them.

We wandered about the city aimlessly, until we spied a massive stadium in the distance.

"That place is as big as Croke Park," Aodhan said. "It must be where the soldiers practice."

"Want to have a look inside?" I asked.

"Are we allowed to do that?"

I shrugged. "If we're not, I'm sure they'll tell us to move on. Come on, what harm can it do?"

"I suppose Scáthach can get us out of any trouble we find ourselves in," Aodhan said, and we headed toward the stadium. There were two guards posted at either side of the entrance, but they only nodded to us as we walked inside. While I was wondering if they knew who we were or if they were just polite to everyone, we emerged onto the stands. The corridor had brought us to a walkway halfway up the rows of seats, and to Aodhan's delight, companies of soldiers were performing training movements on the field below.

"It's like MacCreehy's lot, but these soldiers probably aren't evil," Aodhan said.

"Or under a madman's spell," I added, since MacCreehy had manipulated others into joining his cause. "I'm sure all these people are here of their own free will."

"And look at those swords," Aodhan said, as the weaponry below flashed silver in the sunlight. I leaned to the side, trying to get a look at the person shouting orders, when I caught a glimpse of bright hair on the sidelines.

Kelsey was sitting at the edge of the training field. If she was here, that meant that Kevin must be close by.

"Kelsey," I yelled. She stood up at once, turned around and found me. Kelsey shouted my brother's name and called out my location, as she ran up the stairs toward me. While I watched her take the steps two at a time, Kevin emerged from one of the many entrances on the landing and barreled down the aisle, then he grabbed me in a mighty hug.

"Meri, Meri, Meri," Kevin said, as he squeezed the life out of me. "Dammit, I'm so fecking glad you're all right."

"I was so worried they'd get you, too," I said as I squeezed him back. Many siblings bickered, and some outright hated each other, but not Kevin and me. I had adored my brother since the day I was born, and would do absolutely anything for him. I knew he'd do the same for me. "What did you do with the one they gave you?"

"You mean that ugly bracelet?" he asked. "I handed it over to Ma. No idea what she did with it." He drew back to get a look at me, then Kelsey reached us, panting and red faced and grinning from ear to ear. Kevin looped an arm around her, and we had a proper group hug.

"Bet you never thought you'd be glad to see me," Kelsey teased, but there were tears on her cheeks.

"Bet you never thought you'd cry over the school weirdo," I teased back, as I wiped her cheek with the corner of my sleeve. "Are you two joining up with the soldiers?"

"We've been coming by to watch the morning maneuvers," Kevin replied, then he loosed his arm from Kelsey and brought Aodhan into our massive embrace. "Auntie thinks that after a bit of training, we'd be good instructors."

"Did you just refer to Scáthach, the legendary Shadow, as Auntie?" I asked.

"She is our aunt," Kevin said, but Aodhan shook his head.

"Gotta side with Meri on this one," Aodhan said. "Scáthach does not give off auntie vibes."

"You side with Meri on everything, anyway," Kevin said.

"As he should," Kelsey added, with a meaningful look at Kevin. "Did you guys really drive all across the island to get here?"

"Isn't that how you traveled?" I asked. "Or did you take a boat?"

"Neither," Kevin replied. "We went down to Kilstiffen, then we took a magic sound tunnel here."

"Kevin helped sing," Kelsey added. "His voice was stunning!"

"Really," I said; Kevin had always been sensitive about what he considered his lack of talent when it came to singing. In reality, he just needed to practice. "Look at you, acting like a merrow."

"Easier to sing along in a chorus than as a solo act," he said, then he changed the subject. Typical. "We weren't in Kilstiffen for very long. We told Grandfather about how you were grabbed off the boat, then he went to round up his allies. The rest of us have been here ever since."

"Are there a lot of allies?" I asked. "More importantly, does Ker Ys have many?"

"We can show you," Kelsey said, then she grabbed my hand and led me back through the corridor we'd emerged from, and down into the bowels of the stadium as Kevin and Aodhan followed.

"What's down here?" I asked.

"There's a map of all the sea kingdoms," she replied. "It matches the one your grandfather manages in Kilstiffen. Kevin already learned how to work it."

I leaned toward Kelsey, and murmured, "You're really helping him tap into his abilities. Well done."

"I'm not doing anything," she demurred, as her cheeks darkened. "It's all Kevin. He's amazing, and powerful, and he just needs to accept it."

"All true, but you're there for him. He's always needed a partner to lean on, much like how I lean on Aodhan." I squeezed her hand. "I'm glad it's you."

She glanced sidelong at me. "Really?"

"Really."

Kelsey grinned at me, then she indicated a massive wooden doorway that had a set of hinges running up one side, but no handle. "The map's through here. You can open the room."

"I can? But there's no doorknob."

"It's attuned to our family," Kevin said, as he placed his hand on the door. A moment later, we heard a latch release, then the door swung open, and we entered the room. Along the far wall was a tapestry that depicted not only the Atlantic Ocean in its entirety, but all of the waterways in the world. The seas and oceans were dotted with glowing blue, white, and yellow orbs.

"This is bonkers," Aodhan said, as he approached the map. "These lights. Do they represent all of the other kingdoms?"

"Correct," Kevin said. "Blue lights are with Kilstiffen, and the yellow are for Ker Ys."

"And the white?" I asked, because that was the most prevalent color.

"They're either undecided, or choosing to remain neutral," Kevin said. "Some of the neutral lands I understand, like this one." He pointed to a white orb on the western edge of South America. "It's mad far, and they don't have any current trade agreements with us or Ker Ys. Them staying out of it seems like a wise move, for now."

"And what of the closer undecided lands?" I asked.

"Ah. See this?" He indicated a flickering white orb near the southern tip of Greece. "That's Pavlopetri. They've had a relationship with Kilstiffen for thousands of years, and they've yet to pick a side."

"Do they also have a relationship with Ker Ys?" Aodhan asked. "Perhaps they're caught in the middle."

Kevin scoffed. "If that's the case, they'd best make up their minds quickly. Grandfather sent out the call to all of his allies, and he's not going to forget those who don't respond."

"What about the council?" I asked, since they seemed to have started it all.

"You didn't know? Grandfather expelled them from Kilstiffen. They're not welcome among our allies, either."

That the council was now homeless pleased me greatly. "I suppose that means their dream of recreating Atlantis is off the table."

"At Kilstiffen it is," Kevin replied, "but Corentin has since offered them Ker Ys."

"That's daft," I said. "Ker Ys is bankrupt."

"True, but we believe that's where the plan to snatch you and me came in," Kevin explained. "Grandfather suspects that Corentin wanted to ransom us, and drain Kilstiffen's treasury in the process."

I shook my head. "Corentin never mentioned ransom. He said he wanted Kilstiffen, and that he'd use me to get it... Although, he stated that he needed you, too."

"Huh." Kevin rubbed his chin. "Then they're planning an invasion."

"Invasion? How'd you leap to that conclusion?" I asked.

"A lot of the inner workings in Kilstiffen require the presence of our family in order to operate," Kevin said. "Just like how the door to this room is attuned to us."

"It's not like you two are the only living family members," Aodhan said, but Kevin shook his head.

"True, but we are the most vulnerable," Kevin said. "I don't think anyone could abduct our mother or Scáthach, and Oscar's a ghost. If Corentin's big plan involved me and you, he must need something done below that only we can accomplish."

"I wonder what that could be." I located Kilstiffen on the map, and touched my fingers to the glowing blue light. It was so vast, and I'd never thought of it as anything but safe underneath the waves. Now, I worried it could all be destroyed before I ever really got to know it, or its people. "We saw Dahut on the drive up to the Causeway. I wonder where she is now."

Behind me, Kelsey swore, then she and Kevin exchanged a few quiet words.

"It's nearly time for breakfast," Kevin said to Aodhan and me. "Around here they serve a big meal in the middle of the morning that's more like a brunch. Come on, Aodhan, you'll love it."

With that, Kevin kissed Kelsey's hair, then he led us out of the map room. Aodhan followed, but I paused to glance at Kelsey. She was fuming.

"Why so mad?" I asked.

"I'm not mad," she bit off. "I'm irritated that Dahut keeps turning up, and Kevin thinks I'm overreacting."

"Kevin has no interest in her," I said. "You can trust him."

"I do trust him, and I know he doesn't care about her. It's her that I don't trust." Kelsey looked at me, then away. "Listen, Sarah and I were the meanest, sneakiest people on the planet. I see all of that in Dahut. She can't be trusted. She's a threat, is what she is."

"I believe you," I said. "It's why I kept her from coming here. I only told her to go to Kilstiffen because Grandfather can handle her."

"You told her to go back to Kilstiffen?"

"Back? What do you mean?"

"You know how Kevin and I went down to Kilstiffen before we came here," she began. "We weren't there for very long, only a few hours. When we got to the gates, Dahut was already on her way out."

"Really? No one else mentioned that."

"I doubt anyone else saw her," Kelsey said.

"Did you talk to her?"

"Yeah. Kevin was friendly and polite, and didn't mention that you were missing, and she didn't act like she was up to anything. But you've got to admit, the timing is interesting."

"Almost like she was creating an alibi for herself," I said, and Kelsey nodded. We walked for a bit, then I said, "Down in the caves, where they kept me. Nahel was there."

"Did he hurt you?"

"No, but I hurt him, when I escaped." I slowed down, because I didn't want Aodhan or my brother to hear what I said next. "He had... he had plans for me. Told me all about it."

"Plans? Like, for attacking Kilstiffen."

"No." I squeezed my eyes shut, and said, "Like, in the bedroom."

"Sick bastard," Kelsey said. "Ker Ys is full of them. How do they have any allies?"

"That's a great question," I said, because why did a bankrupt city led by a greedy, incompetent king have so many friends? "I wonder how we can find the answer."

AVIAN SPIES AND PARLOR TRICKS

Our morning meal was held in one of the large Romanesque buildings set on the plateau near the city's center. The food was served on a sunny terrace that was open to a garden, complete with fountains and benches and paths that wound between the multitudes of blooming plants. Ever since I'd known about Evonium and its military leanings I'd imagined it as a utilitarian, Spartan place, but everywhere I looked nature was entwined with and enhanced the manmade objects. I liked that.

Something else I liked was the casual atmosphere on the terrace. Most of the merrow side of my family was in attendance, and we all behaved as if this was a regular meal shared on a regular day, and we weren't three quarters of the way to war.

Also in attendance was a tall, blond, bearded man named Fionn. Scáthach introduced him as her partner in the academy's training programs. Based on the way they spoke while they stood so close to one another, and the small jokes and glances they shared, he was her partner in other things, as well.

"Should I call him Uncle Fionn?" I asked my mother.

"Fionn would appreciate that, but Scáthach might stab you," Mama replied. "Even to our own mother, she's only ever admitted that he helps her with the academy. It's quite similar to how you once denied how much you adore Aodhan," she added.

"That's not fair," I said, aghast that my own mother would say such a thing.

"I was aiming for honesty, not fairness. But if you'd like some fairness, I will admit that at first, I denied what I felt for your father. It was only for a few days, but it felt like forever."

"I suppose there's worse family traits we could share." I sat on the edge of a fountain and held a mug of tea in my hands. Mama sat beside me, and we watched the city spread below us. "Kevin told me he gave you his bracelet that he got from the council?"

"Aye, that he did, and I handed it off to my mother," she replied. "We didn't have time to unwind the bracelet's spells before we came here, and we couldn't risk our enemies using it to lock on to our location."

"Can they even do that?"

"I don't know, but such magics do exist. So, my mother took it below, mostly to pick apart the spells that powered it, but also to throw anyone tracking us off our scent, so to speak."

I sipped my tea, and recalled Kevin's idea from the map room. "Kevin thinks Ker Ys might be planning to invade Kilstiffen."

"Hmm." Mama tapped her chin, then she called over my aunt. When Scáthach and her *partner*, Fionn, were with us, she asked, "What do you think about Ker Ys attempting an invasion of Kilstiffen?"

Scáthach snorted, which clearly delighted Fionn. "I think the very notion is daft, but Corentin was never known for his brains," she said. "I fear Brian beat out whatever sense the boy was born with long ago."

"True, but invasion is still a possibility," Fionn said, in his deep voice that reverberated around us like a bass drum. "According to Meri's report, Corentin and many of his followers are already below. They could infiltrate the city through the caves, a few at a time."

"Kilstiffen's guard would stop them," Scáthach said.

"You only need one or two good warriors to slip in undetected, then they can begin to topple the kingdom," Fionn said. "How many times have we done exactly that?"

Scáthach and Mama shared a glance, then my mother said, "We need to send a warning," Mama said. "To Oscar, Father, everyone."

"Or we could not send anything, and do something unexpected," I said. "Are the caves the only way they could sneak in?"

"While the city remains below, yes," Mama said.

"What happens to the caves when the city is above?"

"The caves reconfigure themselves," she replied. "The routes change, and to my knowledge there are no maps of the tunnels' path after they've changed, save for what a few individuals have committed to memory. If you went into the caves when the city was above, and you weren't expecting the changes, you'd be lost."

"Also, the city has more defenses when it's above," Scáthach added. "The royal navy, for one."

"Then we should definitely raise the city," I said. "It will be safer that way, and if anyone was already moving through the caves, we would effectively trap them."

"That would be terrifying to anyone caught in them unawares," Fionn said. "To have the very ground reorganize itself around you is the stuff of nightmares."

"Nothing less than they deserve," I muttered.

"Meri, I do agree with your plans," Mama began, "but even though the golden key has been returned, Kilstiffen won't rise for another six years."

"That can't be the only way it rises and falls," I said. "Isn't there anything else we can do?"

My mother opened her mouth, no doubt to tell me there was no way my plan would work, when Scáthach said, "Meri could sing it aloft, with the pearl."

I clutched my pendant. "Does the pearl influence the city?"

"No, it influences the wearer," she replied. "Hit the right notes while wearing it, and you can draw on the power of the Tuatha Dé Danann."

"I sang constantly while I was imprisoned," I said, the memory of those cold, dark days making my voice waver. "Why didn't the pearl give me an extra push then, when I needed it more than anything?"

"Perhaps that was due to the caves, as well," Aodhan said. He'd wandered over behind Scáthach and Fionn, no doubt curious as to what we were discussing. "The bedrock on the west coast of Ireland is predominantly limestone, which is a notoriously bad conductor of electricity. Stands to reason it could be a bad conductor of magic, too."

"That makes sense," I said. "When I was down there everyone kept saying how merrows are almost powerless in the caves, and Oscar said that the council's been using that area as a prison for a long time. What better place to stick your prisoner than some place that automatically weakens them?" I turned to Aodhan, and asked, "How did you know that the bedrock is limestone?"

"I waited in that cave for you for six days," he said, my heart clenching at the pain in his voice. "The gift shop has all these books and brochures on the local area, and I read them to pass the time. I'm practically a geologist, now."

"Aodhan, your agile mind has helped us once again," Mama said. "And Meri, we'll do as you suggested."

"We will?"

"Aye," Mama said. "We'll raise the city, keep our people safe, and give Corentin the fright of his life, all at the same time. Though, I suppose someone should warn the king before we get started."

Preparations to raise Kilstiffen began as soon as the breakfast dishes were whisked away. Soon enough, I learned that even though we fully intended to bring the city to the surface, we weren't planning to send Evonium's army there.

"But who will protect Kilstiffen from Corentin?" I asked my mother. We were headed back to our family's tower, where she was going to collect her weapons and a few other items. Aodhan remained with Fionn so he could assist with battle plans, which suited him. Athletes and warriors shared many common traits.

"Kilstiffen can protect itself quite well," Mama replied. "Worry not for them. As for where we're headed, Scáthach's just deciphered Oscar's latest message. It seems that Ker Ys's own forces are mustering near their city in the English Channel. We'll meet the enemy there."

"How does Oscar know so much?" I wondered. "He's everywhere and nowhere at the same time."

"No one knows how Oscar gets his information. Sometimes, I wonder if Oscar understands it himself." We entered her and Da's apartment, which was on the first floor of the tower.

"Why are these your rooms?" I asked. "I assumed you would want the top floor."

"Scáthach and your 'Uncle' Fionn claimed that floor some time ago," Mama replied. "Fionn likes to tend the rooftop garden, when he's not beating down his opponents. But these rooms serve me quite well, and if there's a fight I'll get to it faster without having to come down so many flights of stairs."

"And you'll get there faster than your sister," I added.

"Why, I hadn't thought of that," Mama said, in a tone that made it plain that had been her idea all along. She strode across the front room, which was a much more lived-in version of Aodhan's and my apartment upstairs. As I took in the various details, from the homey rugs and cushions in my mother's favorite colours of burnt orange and soft rose, to the tiny mementos scattered about on small tables and shelves, and I realized something.

"Is this where you stayed after Oscar rescued you?" I asked.

"What makes you ask that?" she asked, trying and failing to sound nonchalant.

"You're everywhere here." I picked up a cowrie shell, put it back down. "And it takes a while to accumulate this much... stuff."

"You're correct on all counts, Meri." Mama leaned against the arched doorway that led to the bedroom. "After Oscar brought me here, he went to Kilstiffen and retrieved Talia so she could assist in my recovery. It was her idea to begin filling this space with small, soft things that reminded me of better days."

"Did her plan work?"

"Aye, it did, though my daily sparring sessions with Scáthach helped just as much, if not more."

"I'm sorry I wasn't here to help you."

"Och, Meri girl, there's nothing for you to be sorry about," she said. "You were a wee thing at the time, and not to be troubled by your mother's problems."

"That's where you're wrong," I said. "Trouble me whenever you need to, about anything and everything. What's the point behind having a family if we can't be here for each other?"

Mama smiled. "And I am always here for you, my lamb." She picked up the sword Manannán had given her at the vow renewal.

"I've only had this a week, yet it feels like I received it a lifetime ago," Mama said.

"It's been quite the week," I said. "The sword is called Fragarach?"

"It is. The name means The Answerer. When Fragarach's blade is at a person's throat, they cannot move, nor tell a lie." She secured the sword into a sheath that lay across her back, and buckled her usual blade around her hips. "When I have Corentin at the end of my blade, I mean to ask him who's truly behind these mad schemes. I doubt that fool created these plans on his own."

"You might not get a chance to ask him," I said. "After I told Aodhan how Corentin beat me—"

"Corentin did what to you?" Mama asked.

I went still. "Please don't swear you'll kill him. I know he deserves punishment, but I don't want you to carry the burden of having killed him."

Mama set her hand on my cheek. "Meri, you are kind and generous, and I am proud to be your mother. I promise you, I will not kill him." She patted my cheek, then she drew back and added a few more knives and other weapons about her person. "Death is far too lenient of a sentence for him. He will be punished, as will those awful twins."

I swallowed, but Corentin had earned his fate. At least it wouldn't be death. "Nahel definitely deserves whatever he's got coming. You don't trust Dahut, either?"

"I don't. If she's truly changed, then it's on her to prove herself." Having finished arming herself to the teeth, she picked up a bag and tossed in a few items. "As for her and Nahel, I suspect we'll end up sending them north, to face that side of their family."

"You don't think they should be punished, like Corentin?"

"I do, but they're descended from the Norse gods. I'd hate to act in a way that angered their family, and caused more problems for us down the line."

"Yes, I see how less problems would be ideal." Since Mama had collected everything she needed from her apartment, we left the tower. Once outside, I said, "You haven't yet explained how we're getting these messages to Grandfather."

She pointed to an area on the far side of the central plateau. "See that obelisk? Atop it is a horn. That's what Scáthach will use to alert Kilstiffen of our plan."

"Wouldn't it be easier to use a cell phone?"

"Perhaps, but there are no telephones of any sort in the city, and would they really get any reception under the sea?" she countered. "As soon as the message is sent, we'll get into position to begin our song. You will take the lead, being that you're wearing the pearl, and Scáthach, Kevin, and I will act as your chorus."

"You can wear the pearl if you'd like," I said in a rush.

"Meri. You can do this."

I swallowed, and looked toward the plateau. I saw Aodhan standing next to Fionn, and Da where he sat with Kevin and Kelsey. Scáthach was near the base of the obelisk, and a familiar man was standing next to her.

"Is that Oscar?" I asked. Mama shielded her eyes against the sun, then she grinned.

"Good eyes, Meri," Mama said. "Let's greet him, shall we?"

We returned to the plateau, where Oscar was sipping tea and wolfing down a plate of food from the breakfast buffet. When he saw Mama and me, he set everything aside to embrace us.

"My wee sister," he said, as he hugged Mama. "Aoife, you look as well as ever."

"As do you," Mama said. "Thank you, for finding Meri."

"It was no trouble," Oscar said, then he faced me. "I imagine you prefer Scáthach's food over what I fed you."

"It was the best soup and biscuits I've ever had," I said. "Will you be helping us raise the city?"

"I suppose I will. Scáthach told me about your mad plan."

"Think it will work?" Mama asked.

"It has potential. Luckily, I came bearing gifts that will help things along." He stepped aside, and revealed two swords, and a large leather case.

"After I parted ways with Meri and Aodhan in the caves, I dipped down to Tir na nÓg, and grabbed a few things from my stash," he began. "The swords are called Moralltach and Beagalltach."

"Greater Fury and Lesser Fury," Scáthach translated. "These swords haven't been seen in an age."

"That's because no one was looking for them inside my storeroom," Oscar said, then he picked up the leather case and withdrew a harp. The frame was gilded, and the strings were shining silver filaments that caught the light. "This harp can enchant people to follow the music wherever it leads. I'm hoping we can use it to distract a fair few of Ker Ys's soldiers."

"It's not like enthrallment, is it?" I asked, recalling Seamus Mac-Creehy's zombiefied army.

"No, because the harp's music won't override someone's free will," he replied. "Instead, it piques their curiosity. Those listening will suddenly be fascinated by the song, and follow it to its source."

"Interesting. Does it do anything else?"

"What, that's not enough?" he asked with a wink, but he answered me, anyway. "The strings never need tuning, and they always sound as sweet as honey." Oscar glanced at his elder sister, and added, "It does have another aspect, but you need to see it to believe it. Fionn, give Scáthach a kiss."

Fionn appeared to be all for it, but Scáthach demanded, "What the devil for?"

"The harp can transform kisses into birds," Oscar replied, as he strummed the harp. "Then we can send the birds off as spies."

"Is that so?" Scáthach glanced at Fionn, and gave him the barest of nods. He leaned in and pecked her cheek, then a tiny grey bird appeared in the air above their heads.

"Amazing," I said. "And the bird will do as you say?"

"Aye, Meri, that it should." Oscar faced the bird, and said as he continued strumming the harp, "Go to Ker Ys, then return and tell me all that you see." The bird chirped a reply, and flew off toward the south. I hoped it wouldn't get lost.

"Now that we've seen a few of your parlor tricks," Scáthach began, her cheeks still dusted in pink, "let's get this message sent to Father. I'd hate to be the one explaining to him why we moved his city without warning him first."

"Here's something I don't understand."

My mother's gaze slid toward me. "What's that?"

She and I, along with Aodhan and Da, were standing off to the side of the obelisk while we watched Scáthach and Oscar use the magic horn to warn Kilstiffen of its coming time in the sun. Fionn also monitored them from his post at the base of the obelisk. I had no idea where Kevin and Kelsey had gotten to.

"If it's possible to sing Kilstiffen above the waves, why have they been hanging out underwater for all this time?"

"Ah." Mama glanced at Da, and continued, "Well, the answer to that, is that Kilstiffen is founded on tradition. The key is what's supposed to make the city rise and fall, and that's the way they like it."

"But it can be raised by song," Aodhan said. "Merrows have done this before?"

"Oh yes. Before the key was created a merrow's song was the only way to move the city."

"You mean to tell me they've been down there, complaining about the lack of sunlight, when they could have raised the city all along?" I shook my head. "This is the same sort of mindset that led to them following the council's advice, isn't it?"

"You're not wrong, Meri," Mama said, as Da muttered something under his breath. "The king tries to instill a more modern way of life in his people, but it's a difficult task when everything around you is steeped in ancient magic."

"As is the rest of Ireland," I said. "Yet you won't find me going around asking fairies to fix my shoes."

Behind me, Da and Aodhan laughed. Mama shot them a good natured glare, then she turned back to the obelisk. "Scáthach and Oscar are headed this way."

"Does that mean the message was a success?" I asked.

My mother held out her hand. "We'll know soon enough," she said, as Da laced his fingers with hers and they walked toward the other two. I moved to follow them, until Aodhan placed his hand on my shoulder.

"How are you doing?" he asked. I turned to him, and burrowed into his arms.

"Better now," I said, as he kissed my hair. "I don't want to go to war."

"Neither do I, but I don't think we have a choice in the matter."

"I thought you wanted to deliver a sound beating to Corentin."

"As satisfying as that would be, I really just want you to be safe." Aodhan tilted up my chin. "No matter what, I'm not leaving your side."

"Good. There is no way I could do this without you." I watched the adults talk about the messages that had been sent and received, and realized that Aodhan and I were adults now, too. That thought was very nearly as terrifying as the coming fight. "How many times have we faced monsters together?"

"A few. Why don't I feel like we're getting good at dealing with these threats?"

Before I could reply, my mother beckoned us to her. "The king agrees with our plan," she said, once we were close enough. "In fact, we'll be helping him along. Once the city is aloft half the navy will sail to Ker Ys, the king included. The remaining ships will guard the city from whatever stragglers emerge from the caves."

"Then should we be on our way to Kilstiffen?" When my mother and aunt looked at me like I'd grown another head, I added, "Don't we have to go there in order to raise it?"

"Actually, no," Scáthach said. "Thanks to my dear brother, we can raise the city right here in Evonium."

RAISING KILSTIFFEN

We assembled on the far side of the plateau to begin our song; apparently, everything of import in Evonium took place on this rocky shelf. Regardless, this side of the plateau soared above the sea, and that proximity to the sea was crucial to our plan succeeding. Our plan being to raise Kilstiffen, that is.

And what a plan it was. Apparently, the harp Oscar had dragged up from the depths was able to create an image of whatever object our song was focused on, regardless of distance. The object in question could be as small as a plum, or as grand as an entire island—or sea kingdom, for that matter. What's more, any action directed at this image—including our song—affected the true object. Oscar had never attempted creating such a large rendering before, but he was confident it could be accomplished, as long as enough merrows sang in concert with him.

But before we could begin singing or strumming, Mama and Scáthach had to discuss and re-discuss where each one of us should stand.

"Are you also a merrow?" I asked Fionn. He, Aodhan, and I stood to one side of the pair as they debated the proper locations for us to stand whilst singing. Oscar looked on, amused.

"Sadly, no," he replied. "I'm but a warrior. Once, I fought giants."

"Really? Were there a bunch of mad giants causing trouble in Evonium, and you came here to stop them?" Aodhan asked.

"No, but there was a legend about the greatest living warrior, one who was as swift as she was deadly," he replied. "And so here I came, and challenged The Shadow to a match."

"Who won?" Aodhan asked.

"She hasn't kicked me out yet, so I would say I did," Fionn replied.

"I beat you in that match, and every match we've had since then," Scáthach said as she and my mother approached us. "Stop filling my niece's head with your nonsense. Meri, we'll have you stand right on the promontory."

"All the way at the edge?" I squeaked.

"You'll be right behind Oscar," she added, and I breathed a sigh of relief. I wasn't scared of heights, but having Oscar between me and the long drop to the sea calmed my nerves.

After a bit more instruction, Oscar took his place dangerously close to the cliff, while I stood about half a metre behind him. Aodhan, as always, was by my side. Fanned out behind us were my mother and Da, Scáthach and Fionn, and Kevin and Kelsey. Behind that row was assembled every merrow in Evonium.

"This will be quite the concert," Aodhan said. "When will everything begin?"

"Now is good," Oscar said, and he strummed his harp. A moment later I joined him, as did those behind me. Our voices and the harp's music blended into one sound as it soared across the sea, and beckoned Kilstiffen to rise up from the depths.

Seabirds cawed overhead as the waves churned below. Suddenly, Aodhan pointed at the sea.

"Meri, look!" My gaze followed his outstretched arm, my song never faltering, and I saw a rendering of Kilstiffen made of light, courtesy of the magic imbued in Oscar's harp. The golden roofs and castle spires pushed upward through the waves, until the center of the city was aloft and bathed in sunshine.

"It's working," Oscar yelled. "Just a bit longer, and we'll have all of it!"

I reached inward, past my vocal chords, past my heart and lungs and deeper into my soul. There, at the depths of my being I found where my power began, where it was born and where it flourished. It was strong, and beautiful.

As was I.

I threw my head back as the music leapt out of my throat, swirling and curling around the other merrows as our song gained strength. The ground rumbled beneath me, and I grabbed Aodhan's arm.

"You all right?" he asked.

I nodded without pausing, altering the tune just enough to reassure him. My gaze traveled to the far end of the rendition, and Kilstiffen's palace. Perhaps it was due to its placement at the edge of the city, or perhaps it was due to its vast size, but the palace was reticent to reveal all of itself. Desperate to give the city its best chance to evade the Ker Ysians, I grabbed my pearl with one hand and Aodhan's arm with the other, and gestured for him to sing with us. He did, then I saw Kelsey and my father join in as well. Lastly, Fionn curled his hand around

Scáthach's arm as he began to sing. She covered his hand with her own, his support having made her own voice stronger.

"Another few bars," Oscar called out. "We're nearly there!"

Finally, the palace burst upward from the waves, the golden spires reaching toward the sun. Oscar gestured for us to sing higher, and as we did the last bits of the city crested the sea.

We'd done it.

"The navy," Oscar said, as he pointed toward Kilstiffen's port. "They're launching!"

I hadn't realized the city had a port; then again, I'd only ever been there while it was situated on the sea floor. We watched with bated breath as Kilstiffen's soldiers and sailors filed onto the ships, then sailed away.

"See that one?" Mama asked; she'd run to the cliff's edge as soon as Oscar mentioned the navy. Now she was pointing at the largest vessel. "The one with the massive blue sail. That's Papa's ship."

I'd never head her refer to the king as Papa before. "Is he coming to get us?" I asked.

"He is not," Mama replied. "The king will sail straight to the ene-my."

"Then how will we get to the English Channel?" I asked.

"Fear not, Meri," Scáthach said. "We've got our own ships."

While all of us merrows had been singing the entire kingdom of Kilstiffen aloft, the rest of Evonium's soldiers had been assembling on their city's own navy. Five ships had already departed, but the sixth and largest ship remained in the harbor waiting for us to board.

"This is a fair sight larger than my boat," Da said, as he craned his neck to see the top of the central mast. "Reckon they won't need my help keeping her afloat."

"Nor mine," Aodhan said. "Is there anything we can do to help during the voyage?"

"I'm sure we'll find a way to keep both of you busy," Scáthach said, then she made her way toward the front of the ship. I turned to speak to Aodhan, but only the barest rasp came out of my mouth.

"Don't try to talk," he said; thanks to my epic vocal performance on the promontory, once I stopped singing my utterly ravaged throat had swollen up. As a result, every sound I made was a painful chore. "I'll find you some water."

I shook my head as I grabbed his arm, since water was the last thing I needed. Back on the plateau I drank some, and it had felt like knives scraping down my throat. Just as I started gesturing at Aodhan, and utterly failing to get my point across, Talia approached us.

"Step back for a moment, Aodhan," Talia said. "Let me help."

Aodhan did as told, and Talia placed her thumb and forefinger on either side of my windpipe. "Meri. Breathe," she said. "Give me a deep, deep breath. I know it's painful, but I need you to feel where it hurts."

I inhaled a great breath, wincing at the pain.

"Now that you can feel exactly where the injuries are, you know where to send your energy," Talia continued. "A merrow's magic is not dependent on their voice. We use our songs to direct our magic, but it is always within us."

I followed her instructions and visualized my battered vocal chords. They were red, and angry. I considered what Talia referred to as my magic, and how it would manifest in my throat.

"Blue," Aodhan said, thus proving he really was always listening to me, whether or not I was speaking out loud. "Healing energy should be blue."

I flashed him a smile as I closed my eyes and imagined the blue of a fresh berry, or a just bloomed iris, or a thick wool blanket, covering up and soothing the red welts in my throat. After a few more deep breaths, the pain faded away.

"It does feel better," I said, then I realized that Talia was standing with us on a warship. "Why are you here? We're headed to battle!"

"This won't be my first fight," Talia said, as she gently prodded my throat. "It won't even be my first war. Remember, I go where I'm needed."

"I don't want you to get hurt."

"Sometimes, that can't be helped." Talia patted my cheek, then she moved on to help others. As soon as she stepped away from me, Aodhan was there.

"How do you feel?" he asked, as he held my face close to his. His long fingers were cool, comforting.

"I'm all right," I said, though my voice was still a bit rough. When his brows pinched, I added, "Really. I'm okay."

Aodhan swept his thumbs across my cheekbones, then he pulled me against him. "What you did back there with your voice was amazing," he murmured, "but I know you need time to rest. Please, love, let me do things for you until you're recovered."

"I do love it when you take care of me," I said, and was rewarded with his smile. "Do you know how long we'll be on this boat?"

"I'm not even entirely sure of where we're going," he replied. "Let's find someone better informed than the two of us."

In his ever genial way, Aodhan spoke with a few crew members, and learned that our journey to Ker Ys would take about five hours. He also learned that since we weren't working crew members, our time would be better spent below deck.

"That was the most polite brush off I've ever received," Aodhan said, as we descended to the cabins. One had been earmarked for our use, which was nice. When we entered the cabin, the first thing I saw was a massive bouquet of yellow roses sitting on the central table.

"Aren't these lovely," I croaked, though it wasn't a painful croak. Thanks to Talia's help I was pain free, but sounded like a frog who'd smoked for the last forty years. "But who brings flowers onto a warship?"

"That was my doing." Aodhan rubbed the back of his neck, and continued, "Things have been right awful lately, for everyone but especially for you, and I just wanted you to have something nice before we got stuck in another battle. When you went off with your ma after breakfast I asked Kevin what could be done, and he suggested putting the flowers in our room."

"Did he?" I asked, touched that Aodhan would ask my brother for advice.

"Well, yes, but I remembered when we were setting up for your parents' ceremony, and you said that yellow roses are your favorite." Aodhan selected a rose from the bouquet, and presented it to me. "Also, we get to sleep here for the next few hours."

"Sleep sounds lovely," I said. "I suppose you negotiated lunch for us, as well?"

"I haven't, but surely they'll feed us." Aodhan glanced toward the door, slightly panicked. "Won't they? Surely they won't leave us here to starve for hours."

"I'm sure we'll be looked after."

We spent the majority of the journey to Ker Ys in the cabin, lying together on the small, hard cot as the warship cut through the waves. My voice still didn't sound particularly good, but at least I could speak without pain. I hoped to be fully recovered in a day or two. That didn't bode well for me singing during the coming battle, however I didn't know if there was anything to be done about that. Perhaps I could track down Talia, and ask her for a bit more advice about healing myself.

Kelsey joined us a few hours into our seclusion below deck. Apparently Kevin was off seeing to some task only he could handle, and Kelsey had gotten bored whilst waiting for him. She produced a deck of cards from that massive bag of hers, and I watched as she and Aodhan played poker.

"Why do you haul around all of that stuff?" I asked, as Aodhan added another rose petal to the pile in the centre of the table. They were using the petals as poker chips, so even though I had no idea what was happening in the game, I got to enjoy the fragrance.

"It's an old habit," Kelsey replied. "After my mom left us, I figured it was only a matter of time before she sent me a message and told me where to meet up with her. I didn't know when the message would come, so I always had to be packed and ready to go. But, as we all know, she buggered off for good." When Aodhan and I only stared at her, she added, "Anyway, it's good to be prepared."

"It is," I began, then Kevin barged into the cabin. Unusually for him, he was armed. "Is that a sword you're carrying?" I asked.

"It's Beagelltach," he said. "Ma just gave me a few lessons on how to use it."

"Who ended up with Moralltach?" I asked. "Scáthach? And why didn't we all get lessons?"

"Scáthach has a barbed spear made from—get this—a sea serpent's bones, and you can ask Ma for your own lessons whenever you want." Kevin sat next to Kelsey and kissed her cheek. "As for Moralltach, I think Da claimed it."

The thought of my gentle father wielding the Greater Fury was slightly terrifying. "Any idea where we are?"

"We're due to drop anchor soon. According to those in the know, Ker Ys presents as a sandbar at low tide, and is almost completely engulfed at high tide. Only the very tip of the palace remains visible when the water's up."

Aodhan whipped out his phone and started looking up coordinates; trust the surfer to have an app that tracked tide levels around the world. "According to my GPS, we're close to the Channel Islands. The tide app says the sea should be at its lowest point within the hour."

"We'll get to see the entire city," Kelsey said. "Great."

"Has there been any word from Grandfather's ships?" I asked.

"We should be coming up on them now." Kevin stood, and offered a hand to Kelsey. "Come on. Let's get out of this stuffy room and see what's happening on deck."

We followed Kevin above, and gasped when we got a look at the sea. We could see France's coastline in the distance. The waves were a deep, dark blue, darker than I'd ever seen them at home. There were a few islands far to the left of us—according to Aodhan's phone, that way was north—and up ahead I saw Kilstiffen's navy. The ship with the blue sail—the king's ship—was moving dangerously close to what I initially thought was a lighthouse.

"That'll be the tip of Ker Ys's palace," Kevin said, then a bell tolled. As the sound reverberated around us, waves rolled back from the tower. Kilstiffen's ships were tossed about like so many bath toys, then a steady hum cut through the bell's peals.

"What's that sound?" Aodhan asked.

"It's Kilstiffen's merrows," I said; even though I couldn't sing with them, I understood the song's intent. "They're calming the sea."

Even though merrows' songs had flattened down the waves, the sea was far from safe. Ker Ys's tower sped upward toward the sky, dragging the entire island city out of the water along with it. Whereas Kilstiffen was a long, flat kingdom, Ker Ys was built like a mountain, with layer upon layer of roads and buildings winding around like a massive beehive. Finally, a stretch of sand appeared behind the mountain, long and undulating like a lion's tail.

"Drop anchor," Scáthach called from her place at the bow. "First wave is about to launch! Archers, take your marks!" She saw Kevin and me, and approached us.

"We'll approach in the second wave," Scáthach said. "After the smaller boats launch, we'll swing around and give the archers a clear view."

"Should we wait for the second wave?" I asked. "What if the others need us?"

"The honor of being first to smite our foes goes to the king," Scáthach replied, then she was off to issue more orders.

After Kilstiffen's boats set off and our own ship swung around, I watched as the first vessel landed on Ker Ys's drenched beach. Grandfather was the first of Kilstiffen's warriors to set his foot on the sand, though he didn't look ready for battle. He was wearing his usual getup of green velvet clothes edged in dark fur, and carried a tall wooden staff. He'd even worn his crown of golden shards.

Alone, Grandfather walked across the sand. In that moment he did not resemble the mighty king of Kilstiffen as much as an old man out for a stroll on the beach. My heart was in my throat; surely we weren't going to leave him out there with no reinforcements! Just as I was about to suggest that someone should go out there with him, a horn sounded from the mountainous city.

Ker Ys's cavalry, at least a hundred soldiers all wearing the white horse rampaging across the waves on their tunics, charged toward my grandfather.

Grandfather paused, set his staff in the sand, and sang.

He *sang*.

It wasn't just a song. Waves of pure sound poured forth from his throat and decimated everything in their path.

As for the Ker Ysians, they didn't stand a chance. Grandfather's song knocked them off their feet and pushed them off the beach into the waves where they flailed and floundered. I hoped their armor rusted.

"That is Steinar the Immoveable," Aodhan cheered. "He's amazing!"

"He is," I agreed. We watched as Grandfather unleashed a second song. As he sang his mouth opened wider and wider, his jaw practically unhinged as sound rushed out of him in visible, pulsating waves. The cavalry's second charge was blown back as if a gale force wind was unleashed, with horses foundering and soldiers slipping off the sand bar and into the ocean, and stumbling into the first lot Grandfather had routed.

"Is that it?" I asked, shocked and happy that Grandfather appeared to have defeated an entire army single handedly. "Is it over?"

"Not hardly," Kevin said, then he pointed toward the edges of the sandbar. Waves frothed on either side, and more of Ker Ys's soldiers flowed onto the beach. Grandfather sang a third time, stunning those closest to him, then he hefted his staff and ran headlong into battle, clubbing and striking anyone within reach.

Melodious screams rang out from the opposite side of our ship. As Evonium's soldiers clambered down rope ladders to the waiting boats, the merrows sang until they levitated off the deck and onto the sandbar below. Then my mother, Kilstiffen's champion, leaped off the prow and flung herself into the battle.

"Aoife's always been a bit of a grandstander," Oscar said, as he sidled up to us whilst strumming his harp. He'd no sooner said the words than Scáthach climbed onto the railing and jumped in after her. "And my other sister is no different."

"If Scáthach's in the thick of it, who's minding the ship?" Aodhan asked. Oscar jerked his chin toward the captain's spot, and I saw Fionn ably handling things while my father stood by.

"Officially, Fionn is the captain of the fleet," Oscar replied. "And if he thinks Scáthach needs him, I imagine he'll hand command over to his second."

"What if that one also thinks he's needed in battle?" I asked.

"I'm sure we've a third in command ready to go," Oscar replied, then one of his grey songbirds returned and chirped in his ear.

"What did it tell you?" I asked, then an enormous wave crashed onto the deck. The water pushed me off my feet and clear to the back of the ship. When it subsided, I wasn't near Aodhan or Oscar. Before I could get my bearings, the water rose up again, only this time it wasn't another wave.

Nahel was astride the water, riding it like a horse.

"Little one," Nahel said. "Did you think I wouldn't find you?"

"I was hoping I'd killed you," I rasped. "How's your head? Still hurt?"

"Don't worry, I won't hold your escape against you," he said. "I know that once we're together, you will regret what you did. And there are many, many ways you can make it up to me."

Nahel had the audacity to smile and then wink at me. Fury boiled up from my toes and all the way to the top of my head, and I opened my mouth to sing at Nahel with the same fury Grandfather had unleashed on Ker Ys's army.

And croaked.

"What was that?" Nahel asked, as the plume of water he was riding lowered him to my level. "I didn't hear you. Say again?"

I opened my mouth, but he grabbed my throat and lifted me up off my feet. "Now that you've got no cave to hide in, or voice to push me away, we can finally get to know one another."

Nahel tightened his grip on my throat, as his other hand lifted my shirt. I clawed at his hands as my feet worked, but he was too strong for me. As I reached deep within myself for the dregs of my power, I heard a *thunk*.

Nahel's eyes went wide, then he slumped forward. The wave splashed away, and Nahel's limp form fell onto me and pinned me to the deck.

"Get off, get off," I muttered, then Aodhan shoved Nahel's body aside and pulled me away from him. For a moment I let Aodhan hold me, then I looked at the unusually silent Nahel. He was out cold, and a green crust was forming over his skin.

"What is happening to him?" I asked.

"I threw that green stone from Sionnan at him." With his foot, Aodhan indicated where the stone was lodged in the center of Nahel's back. "I only wanted him to get away from you, but I think this is why Sionnan gave me the stone. It was to help me keep you safe from him."

"She did say she knew what had happened to me in the caves," I murmured, then I realised something. "If Nahel's here, Corentin probably is, too."

Aodhan nodded. "Doesn't look like Nahel's going anywhere," Aodhan said; the green crust that spread across his body was getting thicker, and more opaque. At this rate Nahel would become one with the green stone, and sink to the bottom of the sea. A fitting end, in my opinion. "Let's leave him for now, and find the rest."

We picked our way across the deck, which Nahel had thrown into utter chaos with his entrance. But my aunt's crew was efficient and well trained, and by the time we reached the prow most things had been set to rights.

That was when the sea monster burst forth.

"What the hell is that?" I shrieked.

"That one's like Donn, but female," Aodhan said. The creature was as big as a skyscraper and vaguely female in shape, and she swung an enormous fishing net in an arch over her head. She roared, and caught one of Kilstiffen's ships in her net.

"Archers, release," Fionn ordered, as the trapped ship splintered under the net's weight. A volley of arrows sailed forth, only to pass harmlessly through the sea creature's watery body.

The creature roared and swung her net again, this time at one of Evonium's fleet. Another ship crumbled under the weight of the soaked rope and splintered. Scáthach leapt upon the ship's battered hull, and tried to cut through the net with her barbed spear. The creature jerked the net, and planks flew as Scáthach went under. Fionn bellowed a mighty war cry, and jumped into the ocean after her.

"Aodhan, what are we going to do?" I asked. On the far side of the deck, I saw Da rush toward Kevin. I couldn't see Kelsey or Oscar, then the ship lurched to the side and we lost our balance and slid toward the back of the deck. Aodhan grabbed onto me as a herd of white horses galloped onto the ship.

Not just horses. They were the Camargue, and Dahut was leading them.

"Meri," Dahut yelled. "Get on a horse! They can take you to safety!"

"What about my family?" I demanded.

"They can ride the horses, too," she replied, then the creature's net crashed onto the deck and wood and other debris went flying. I reached for the closest horse, and hoped I wouldn't drown.

THE REAL VILLAIN

I opened my eyes, and saw the sky. That had to be good, right? At least I wasn't in a cave.

Underneath me was cold, wet sand. I tried to sit up; when that didn't work, I rolled onto my side. Next to me were a few of the Camargue, standing around like regular horses, and not the magical, murderous beasts they truly were.

Wait, when did I decide that they're murderous?

No one had mentioned the Camargue being killers; after all, regular horses were vegetarians, and it stood to reason that these horses also preferred hay and grain over meat. But Scáthach had said that the Camargue were formidable adversaries, and her opinion was one I trusted.

In a rush I recalled how she went under the waves, and how the amazingly huge sea monster's equally huge net had destroyed the ship we were on, along with several others. Before I could deal with these horses, I needed to find my people.

"Aodhan?" I croaked. My throat was still ravaged from earlier, and my second near drowning in a week hadn't helped matters. When he didn't respond, I called, "Dahut?"

"I'm here," she said, as she entered my field of vision. With my last bit of strength, I pushed myself upright, and realized we were on the sandbar behind Ker Ys's palace. I craned my neck around and looked past her, and saw Aodhan, my father, and Kevin and Kelsey lying on the sand. They all appeared to be unconscious.

"Are they all right?" I asked. "Where's my mother?"

"Those four are fine," Dahut replied. "The Camargue got them off the ship, as they did you. As for your mother, Aoife remains in the battle."

"We should help her," I began, but Dahut shook her head.

"None of you are in any condition to do that," she said. "I barely got you off the ship before it went down."

She was right, and the five of us weren't fighters to begin with. "Why can't I hear or see the battle?"

"It's on the other side of the island." Dahut swept her arm toward the palace. Now that I was closer to Ker Ys, I could see the massive seawall that stood at the base of the hill, along with the central gate. Unlike Kilstiffen's solid gold entrance, this one was forged from dark iron.

"We should get inside where it's safe," Dahut continued.

"Did anyone else make it off the ship?" I asked. "My uncle was there, and... and Nahel."

Dahut pursed her lips. "I only had time to get you five. As it was, we almost didn't make it."

I nodded. "Thank you. I don't mean to sound ungrateful, and I'm so sorry I didn't trust you at The Shannon."

"It's all right," Dahut said. "You trust me now, don't you?"

"Yes. Of course."

"Good." Dahut smiled tightly, then she offered me a hand up. "Now let's get the others awake and inside, and figure out how we can help everyone else."

One by one, we woke the other four and Dahut told them the same story; the sea monster had destroyed the ship we'd been standing on, and the Camargue had rescued everyone they could. Well, we told three of them the story. Nothing we did roused Kelsey, and Kevin started to panic.

"What if it's a head wound?" Kevin demanded, as he cradled Kelsey in his arms. "We need to bring her to hospital."

"We need Talia," I began, then I remembered that Talia had been on the same ship as us. I swallowed my sob, and asked, "Dahut, are there any healers here?"

"Of course we have healers." She gestured for us to follow her. "Let's go inside and get Kelsey some help."

We followed Dahut across the sandbar, and toward Ker Ys's rather foreboding gate. Da hung back with Kevin, I assumed to help him carry Kelsey.

I stumbled on a piece of driftwood, and Aodhan caught me. "Thank you," I said, but when I would have kept walking, he held me still. "What's wrong?"

"The sea monster that attacked the ship," he began. "Remember way back when you got that bogus betrothal, and your mother was telling us about Dahut and Nahel's family? The Norse side? She said their mother is one of Ran's daughters."

"What does that mean?" I asked.

Aodhan glanced at Dahut, then he replied, "I did some research on Norse legends, and learned that Ran is a sea goddess. She has a special fishing net, and she uses it to pull sailors down to the ocean floor."

"What does she do with the sailors once she has them?"

"Eats them as snacks, hosts a round of golf, who knows," Aodhan said. "Meri, I think Ran attacked our ships."

I gasped, then I remembered something Kelsey had told me whilst we were n Evonium. "Dahut," I called. "Why were you in Kilstiffen before we saw you at The Shannon?"

Dahut stopped walking. "I wasn't."

"You were. Kelsey saw you, and now Kelsey won't wake up." I took a step toward her, and said, "I think you were there to learn about Kilstiffen's navy, and how you could sic your grandmother on them."

"My grandmother—"

"Is Ran," I finished. "What's really happening here? What have you done?"

"All I've done is take back what's mine," she snapped, then the horses circled around us. The Camargue pushed Aodhan and me apart, then one used its teeth to lift me up by the back of my shirt and carry me kicking and screaming into Ker Ys's palace.

Very Much Not Dead

Amazingly, being carried in a giant horse's mouth hadn't added to my injuries in any significant way.

The horse was also unbothered my thrashing and screaming; all my protests had accomplished was to make my already sore throat hurt even more, along with a few minor muscle strains. My equine captor hauled me through the palace gates and up a set of stone steps, then it dropped me onto a cold tile floor. Four more horses stuck their white heads into the room, and similarly dropped Aodhan, my father, and lastly, Kevin and Kelsey into the room.

"Is everyone all right?" Da asked, then he groaned. "Alive, at least?"

"Kelsey's still out," Kevin said, sounding near tears. I dragged myself over to his side. He was sitting up with Kelsey cradled in his arms.

"Do you know why she's out?" I asked. "Did the wave knock her out, or did she get injured a different way?"

"I don't know," Kevin said. "I didn't see her get hurt, but after that wave hit the deck, everything happened so fast."

"Let's look her over," Da said, and between the two of us, we checked her body for wounds.

"She doesn't seem to be bleeding, and nothing appears broken," I said, once we were done. "Do you think Dahut could have done something to her?"

"I don't see how, but yeah. Maybe." Kevin smoothed Kelsey's hair back from her forehead. "She's been wary of Dahut from the beginning, and I just brushed her off. Said she was making problems where there weren't any. I ignored her concerns, and now..."

"You could try healing her," I said, before Kevin's words got any darker. What Kelsey needed right now was help, and hope. There would be time enough for him to feel guilty once this was all behind us. "Oscar taught me that we can heal with our voices."

"Aye, that's true," Da said. "Your ma was trained to tend her own wounds during battle, so she could keep fighting." Da looked toward the open doorway, and the herd of Camargue standing watch in the corridor beyond. He so obviously wanted to get back out there and find Mama, but there was no way we could get past the horses in our current state.

"You know she's still fighting," I said to Da, as I set my hand on his arm. "If anything, she'll make her way to us long before we find our way out of this mess."

Da patted my hand. "You're right about that, and Kelsey's the one who needs us right now. All right, Meri girl, how do we go about healing Kelsey?"

How, indeed. "Kevin, you'll have to try and visualize where she's hurt, and use your voice to undo the injuries," I began, but he shook his head.

"I can't sing well enough for that," he said. "Meri, you need to do it."

"I can't. Believe me, I would help Kelsey in a heartbeat, but I can't. My throat's been gammy ever since we raised Kilstiffen. And you can do this," I added, with such intensity my voice got extra raspy. "Talia told me that a merrow's power comes from within, and we just use our songs to direct it."

"Power," he repeated. "I never thought of me as having power."

"You're the heir of Kilstiffen, and you're a merrow," I said. "You were born with power. You just need to tap into it, and use it to help Kelsey."

Kevin nodded, but he didn't sing. Instead, he continued stroking Kelsey's hair as fat tears rolled off his cheeks and splashed onto her arm. Just when I was going to ask him when he planned on doing something, he started to hum. It was a simple tune that reminded me of a lullaby, but more importantly, Kevin was tapping into the power that lived deep within him. After I got the general feel of the tune, I joined in by tapping my fingers to the beat; since I couldn't sing just yet, it was all I could do. A moment later, Da started in, then Aodhan wrapped his arm around my shoulders and lent his voice, as well. Together, we hummed and tapped for Kelsey.

And hoped. We did a lot of hoping.

Kevin's voice cracked, and he paused to clear his throat. "Kels," he murmured, as he held her face close to his. "Come on, Kels. Please, come back to me."

He rested his forehead against hers, his tears streaming onto her cheeks.

I turned into Aodhan and sobbed, certain Kelsey was gone.

Amazingly, she coughed.

"Kelsey?" Kevin sat up straight, bringing her with him. "Kelsey, love, talk to me. Please."

"Where are we," she mumbled, then Kevin was squeezing her and murmuring in her ear.

"She's okay," I said to Aodhan, relief flooding my voice. "She's going to be okay."

Once we were sure that Kelsey was awake and lucid, and doing as well as she could be for the time being, we took stock of our surroundings. The Camargue had deposited us into a large room with bare stone walls and a tile floor, and there wasn't a window or a stick of furniture to speak of. It was like a civilised version of the cave I'd been stashed in whilst below.

"Amazing, that there's nothing in here but us," Aodhan said. Thanks to his superhuman stamina, he'd been the first one to get up and take a jog around the perimeter. "We don't even have a single shelf or cubby."

"Perhaps not at first glance," Da said, as he followed Aodhan's path with his fingers trailing against the wall. When he felt something interesting, he paused to investigate. "Ah. Here we have a seam." Da traced the near-invisible crack in the otherwise solid wall. "And here is a latch."

Da worried the latch, and a heretofore hidden door popped open. Inside the opening was a cushioned bench long enough to seat eight or maybe ten people, which he pulled out into the room. While it was nice to have something to sit on, it was not the escape route I'd hoped for.

"Kevin, let's get Kelsey up and off the floor," Da said. Whilst he and Kevin settled Kelsey onto the bench, Aodhan and I continued inspecting the wall. We found a few more built-in benches, and a cabinet filled with blankets and extra cushions; I thought the blankets were an odd item to find, but being that we'd all gotten soaked after the ship went down, they were sorely needed. While I brought one of the blankets to Kelsey, Aodhan kept investigating.

"What have we here," he said, as another door popped open. He rooted through the drawers for a moment, then announced, "This is a full sideboard, plates and cutlery included. This must be a dining room of sorts."

"Dining room," I repeated; this place seemed more like an atrium than a place people would sit down to eat. "What sort of cutlery is in there? Are there knives?" I added, with a glance toward the doorway. Ordinarily I wouldn't consider stabbing a horse, but needs must.

"Look for serving forks and spoons," Da called over. "A body could do some damage with one of those."

Aodhan nodded, and started going through the drawers and cupboards as he searched for items we could use as weapons. As he stacked up serving platters along with carving knives and forks, everything made less and less sense.

"Why would Dahut put us in a room that has weapons?" I asked. "Shouldn't we be in a dungeon instead of a dining room?"

"Simple," Kevin said. "She doesn't see us as a threat. In Dahut's mind, she's already won."

"But what has she won?" I muttered. "She's the elder twin, so she would have ruled Ker Ys one day. And I'm sure if she went through the proper channels, our grandfather would have gladly lent aid to help her rebuild everything that Gradlon squandered."

"Gradlon was in deep with the council," Aodhan reminded me. "Maybe Dahut doesn't like the idea of them making Ker Ys into a new version of Atlantis."

"I suppose it could be that simple." I investigated the rear wall of the room, and discovered yet another cupboard. This one was filled with linens.

"Why is everything hidden?" I asked the assorted tablecloths and napkins. "If this is a dining room, why not have a table and chairs? Why not a lovely hutch to display everything? Yet everything here is stuffed into the walls."

Da came up behind me, and had a look at the contents of the cupboard. "This linen is quite fine," he observed, as he rubbed the fabric between his thumb and forefinger. "Makes one wonder why they're hiding their wealth, instead of showing it off. In my experience, royalty prefer to be flashy."

I recalled the fancy meals I'd attended in Kilstiffen, which had featured solid gold forks and centerpieces made of gigantic pearls and gilded coral. "They must owe someone, and they're pretending they're poor so they can put off repayment."

"Aye," Da said. "The question is, who?"

"When I was in the caves, I heard Corentin talking about a plan, but I don't know who he was speaking to," I said. "Whatever this plan was, they needed both me and Kevin to pull it off. Kevin thought it was about invading Kilstiffen, but what if Ker Ys told someone they could hand us over? Although, I'm not sure who would want us," I added.

"Lots of people," Aodhan said. "You're both Kilstiffen royalty, and you're descended from the king of the otherworld."

I opened my mouth to dispute his claims, then I remembered Manannán's appearance at my house, handing out magical gifts and wearing his immense power like a flashy red cloak. "But if we're targets, then Mama and her siblings are, too."

"They are," Da said. "Always have been. Anyone who wants a line to the Otherworld tries to get there through Aoife, and it's the core of the reason why Oscar was sent down to Tir na nÓg. As for Scáthach, while I don't know the exact reason she relocated to Evonium, she has been raising her army for the last thirty years."

I looked toward the sole entry to this room, and the massive horses that were keeping us trapped inside. "We've got to get out of here. They need our help."

"Can you use the pearl?" Aodhan asked, as he nodded toward my pendant. "Ask Manannán for help?"

"Is that wise?" I asked, as I clutched the pearl. "Perhaps if I did that, I would be playing into their hands. Besides, I still can't sing. Kevin," I said, as I turned toward my brother. He was stretched out on the bench, fast asleep with Kelsey gathered against him.

"He loves her so much," I said.

"That he does," Da said. "We should let them sleep for a bit. Actually, we should all rest, and take a moment to figure out our next move."

"Everyone, have a look," Aodhan yelled.

I blinked myself awake; after we'd agreed to let Kevin and Kelsey rest, I'd sat myself on the bench next to theirs and promptly fell asleep. "What are we looking at?" I asked, as I rubbed my eyes.

"This," Aodhan said, as he indicated yet another hidden cupboard. This one was bigger than the others, and seemed to lead to a hallway covered in shelves. "I found the liquor cabinet! We've got wine, what looks like brandy, and some vodka."

I glanced at my father. He shrugged. "Are you planning to have a drink?" I asked.

"Not in the slightest, but what we can do is turn these into bombs," he replied. "There's a drawer full of candles in with the tablecloths. We can make wicks from the linens, seal everything with wax, and toss them at the horses."

"How will we light them?" I asked.

"Kelsey's got like three lighters in her bag," Aodhan said, and I recalled that her bag had made it onto Ker Ys with her. "One of them must be working."

I turned toward the Camargue waiting patiently in the corridor, and wondered if they could understand us. "But then, how will we get out? What with the ensuing fire and all?"

"Well, that's where Kevin comes in," Aodhan said, as he rubbed the back of his neck. "I'm hoping he can sing us a path through whatever destruction we cause, much like how you two sang us through the hedge at the golf course back when we were tracking Donn."

I shook my head. "I don't know."

"I can do it," Kevin said over me. Not only was he awake, Kelsey was too, and she was looking a fair sight better than she had earlier. "If it means we will be getting out of this place, I can do it."

"All right," I said. "Let's make some bombs."

We set up a small assembly line with the liquor bottles, candles, and linens. Da located a corkscrew (this really was a well-stocked dining room) and he opened the bottles while Aodhan shredded the tablecloths into long strips. I stuffed the linen into the bottles, and Kevin carefully melted wax around the bottlenecks to seal them tight. Kelsey observed the production from her perch on the bench, while also keeping an eye on the door. Soon enough, we had our arsenal.

"This should be plenty to get us started," Da said. "We can haul whatever we don't use here back to the fight, and perhaps bomb the opposing army."

I glanced at the Camargue and frowned. "I don't like the thought of hurting the animals."

"Why are we going through the horses?" Kelsey asked.

"It's the only way out," I said.

"Is it?" She pointed toward the back of the wine cabinet. Now that the shelves weren't packed full of bottles, we could see a corridor that stretched behind it, and there was light at the far end.

"Has that always been there?" I peered down the corridor. "Perhaps that's a window?"

"And a window means a way out," Aodhan said, then he grabbed two of the remaining unshredded tablecloths. "Let's pack up these bombs, and go have a look."

Aodhan and Da fashioned the tablecloths into slings, and each of them carried six of the bombs slung over their backs. Kevin dragged the shelves to the side, and the five of us entered the very dark, very dusty corridor. Kelsey and I, wounded as we were, brought up the rear. When she shivered, I put my arm around her.

"Want me to run back for a blanket?" I asked.

"That's okay," she replied. "I just want my clothes to dry out."

"They will," I said, with far more confidence than I felt. My clothes had taken forever to dry when I was imprisoned below, and since the battle on the sea was most likely still underway, I had a feeling we'd be getting wet again. "Other than damp clothes, how are you feeling?"

"A bit off," she admitted. "I feel dehydrated, if that makes sense." She lowered her voice, and asked, "Did you see the Camargue when they were on the ship?"

"Yes. They rescued us."

Kelsey shook her head. "They're the reason the ship went down. When Kevin and I were near the railing, I saw them approach. The horses beat the hull with their hooves until it came apart, then that water woman used her net to snap it apart."

Up ahead, Da stopped walking. "The horses downed the ship?"

"Saw it with my own eyes," Kelsey said. "I grabbed Kevin's arm to tell him, then the deck tilted, and we fell."

"We need to find Aoife," Da said. "She needs to know who the true enemy is."

"And Grandfather," I said. "And the rest."

Da nodded. "We'll find all of them."

From farther down the corridor, Aodhan called, "We've got a door. The light's coming through a window in the top." He pulled on the large metal handle. "Locked. We can blow it open," he said, as he reached for one of the bombs.

"Not a good idea in such a small space," Da warned. "Effective, though."

"We don't need a bomb," I said, as I stood between him and my brother. "Kevin, sing a low note. Make it an exploratory sound, like the music's having a look inside the lock."

He swallowed, but didn't say he couldn't do it. That was great, because we needed his voice now more than ever. Kevin placed his hand on the door, and let out a higher note than I would have used, but that was all right. It was his song, not mine.

"The door's not locked, at least not with a key," he said. "But there is an internal latch keeping it closed."

"We can handle this," I said. "The note you just sang? Do it again, then lift your voice. Make the latch move with it."

Kevin closed his eyes, and sang for a moment. Out of nowhere, he increased in volume, and the door flew open so fast it banged against the interior wall.

"Good job," Da said, as he patted Kevin's shoulder.

"Yes, very good job," I added, then I looked inside the room. It was a dingy cell, and sitting on a stack of hay bales was the very much not dead king of Ker Ys, Gradlon Mor.

"Have you come to rescue me?" he asked.

IT'S A CELL, NOT A BEDCHAMBER

"We thought you were dead," I blurted out.

"Who told you that?" Gradlon demanded.

"Dahut," I replied. "She said Corentin killed you."

Gradlon sniffed. "Corentin couldn't even manage to—" He caught sight of Da scowling at him. "Let me guess, you're the man Aoife wisely chose to wed instead of my brother?"

"Say my wife's name again, and you'll live to regret it," Da growled. "What's happening in this godforsaken land of yours?"

"What isn't?" Gradlon snapped. "Everyone in my family is committing treason, some in tandem, and some independently." Gradlon's head drooped, and I took in his appearance. The once proud king of Ker Ys had on tattered, filthy clothing instead of the regal jewels and furs he usually wore. Based on the state of his cell, illuminated by a single barred window, he'd been in here for a while.

Perhaps he'd been locked in this cell right around when I got stuck in a cave.

"Who put you in here?" I asked. "Dahut or Nahel?"

Gradlon scoffed. "Nahel can barely put his shoes on, but he adores his uncle—who, incidentally, is also brainless. Those two couldn't conjure a puddle in a rainstorm." He frowned, and added, "It's Dahut you should be wary of."

"We noticed," Aodhan said. "Dahut and her horses destroyed the ship we were on."

"And Ran decimated the rest of our fleet," Kevin added.

Gradlon stilled. "Ran attacked your fleet? You're certain?"

"Ran's a tall water woman with a big scary net?" Aodhan asked, and Gradlon nodded. "Yeah, that was her."

"Where is this decimation taking place?" Gradlon asked.

"Right outside the palace," I replied. "Your brainless brother has incited a full naval skirmish between Ker Ys, Kilstiffen, and Evonium."

"Fool," Gradlon hissed. "But that doesn't explain why you lot are here."

"The Camargue dropped us in an empty room," I replied. "We found a hallway behind a hidden liquor cabinet, followed it, and found you."

"Instead of leaving this place altogether, you snooped behind cabinets?" he demanded.

"The Camargue are blocking the way out," I snapped. Gradlon had to be the most ungrateful man ever rescued.

"Well, then I'll just tell them to move," Gradlon said. "They are bound to obey their king."

Gradlon strode out of the cell, with me close behind. "I thought they were bonded to Dahut," I said.

"The Camargue are bonded to all of us," he replied. "Every member of the royal family undergoes the bloodletting ritual on their eighth birthday." Gradlon glanced at me, and added, "Nahel cried during his bloodletting. Dahut did not."

"Neither of those facts surprise me," I said, then I heard the sound of stone scraping against stone. At the end of the hallway, someone was dragging the door closed.

"Hey, wait," Aodhan yelled, but whomever was closing the door either didn't hear him, or was trapping us on purpose. "Kelsey! Lighter!"

Kelsey tossed one of her many lighters at Aodhan. He caught the lighter one-handed, ignited it, and traced the edge of the door with the flame's light. "No handles or latches on the inside," he announced. "Not that I thought there would be."

"Did you see who shut us in?" Da asked.

"No." Aodhan snuffed the lighter, and tossed it back to Kelsey. "Kevin, can you unlatch it?"

My brother approached the door, and set his hand on the seam. He sang for a minute or so, then he shook his head. "There's no latch or handle to speak of, and the seam's become filled with mortar. That means this doorway was likely closed by magic."

"How did you open it in the first place?" Gradlon asked.

"When we opened the liquor cabinet, the doorway was already open," Aodhan replied. "The door must have been off to the side, and we didn't notice it in the darkness."

"Or it was warded to remain unnoticed," I added, then I turned to Gradlon. "Can we get out through your cell?"

"Obviously not," Gradlon said. "It's a cell, not a bedchamber."

"How were you brought to the cell?" I asked. "Was it also through this cabinet?"

"No," he sneered. "I climbed up through the floor."

I was a bare second from telling Gradlon to answer my questions properly, but Da was already inside the cell and investigating the floor. "There's a trap door here," he yelled. "It's closed tight now. Must be locked from the other side."

Kevin pushed past me, then he went down on his knees as he sang to unlock the trap door.

"Why aren't you singing?" Gradlon asked. "Aren't you the one who inherited Steinar's legendary voice?"

My throat tightened when he mentioned Grandfather, but I didn't want Gradlon to realise how strongly his words had affected me. "I strained my voice earlier, when we raised Kilstiffen."

"You raised an entire kingdom with a song?" Gradlon demanded. "What possessed you to attempt such a thing?"

"Actually, we did it to trap Corentin in the caves beneath the city." I glanced at Gradlon, and debated how much I should tell him. Could this bitter man actually be on our side? Since my allies were dwindling faster than my patience, I decided to go for broke.

"A little more than a week ago, Corentin sent me an enchanted bracelet, and ended up abducting me and imprisoning me in the council's prison block," I said. "As far as we knew, when we raised Kilstiffen he was still down there. Now, I suspect he might be here."

"The council adores that cave system, which proves how foolish they truly are," Gradlon said. "They've been trying to invade Kilstiffen for decades, but they make their home base right under Steinar's nose. As if he doesn't know everything that happens in and around his kingdom."

"If you knew all of this was happening, why didn't you say anything?" I asked. "When we met you, you were acting like you were Grandfather's friend."

"I didn't say anything, because everyone knows what the council has been planning," Gradlon replied. "Steinar has always kept them in check, until now."

"I wonder what changed," I murmured. I hadn't expected Gradlon to answer, but he did.

"You and your brother are what changed things," he began. "Years before, Steinar's firstborn left Kilstiffen to run an academy, then his son retreated below. When his youngest child, your mother, went and committed what seemed to be the ultimate treason, the council thought they could isolate Steinar and wear him down. They might have done it, too, but then your brother was born, which meant Steinar once again had an heir. And then you came along, and he had a second heir."

"We were babies," I began, but he held up his hand.

"Royal babies, who have the blood of the Tuatha Dé Danann running through their veins. You not only had a powerful lineage, you had power you were born with that no one could take from you, not even the council. Shortly after your births, the councillors realized they would never claim Kilstiffen as theirs, and they began to look for other kingdoms."

"And so they went to Corentin."

Gradlon sighed, and for a moment he looked like a tired old man. "Yes. They whispered in my brother's ear, told him everything he wanted to hear and not one word of the truth."

Kevin bellowed the last of his song as metal snapped, then Da hauled open the trap door. Beneath it was a rickety wooden ladder and absolutely no light.

"I take it that's the only way out?" Da asked.

"Sadly, you are correct," Gradlon replied.

Kelsey groaned, then she handed one of her lighters to Aodhan, and another to Da, while keeping one for herself. Thus armed, we descended into the darkness.

SALT MINES AND SELKIES

The ladder turned out to be stronger than it looked, which was good. What wasn't good was the cold, dark, cramped tunnel it led to. None of us could walk upright, not even me. That, and the fact that all of this seemed a little too familiar.

"Is anyone else reminded of the tunnel beneath the golf course that led to Aodhan's shop?" I asked.

"I could stand up straight in that tunnel," Kevin grumbled. "But yeah, this is the same deal. Does that mean Donn's involved?"

"My association with Donn ended when you stole my salt," Gradlon replied. When I gasped, he continued, "Are you surprised by my candor? I thought you of all people would appreciate it, heiress."

"I didn't set out to steal your salt," I began, more irritated at Gradlon referring to me as heiress than him calling out my theft. "Donn was gearing up to kill my mother, and I thought your salt was the only way I could stop him. I only wanted to borrow a bit. Dahut said she would speak to you, and explain what had happened," I added.

"As we now know, Dahut has her own agenda," he said. "But you were correct. There are precious few ways to halt a rampaging god, and Ker Ys's salt is one of those ways. Pity we don't have any left. It would come in handy now."

"Maybe if you hadn't gotten in with Donn in the first place," I began, then I heard Da cry out as his lighter went dark. "Are you all right?"

"Just burnt myself a wee bit," he replied. "I'm fine, just a bit singed."

"When you were brought into your cell, was it this dark?" Aodhan asked, as he angled the lighter toward the tunnel walls. "No torches, no anything?"

"I don't know how things are done in the surface world, but here we rarely consider the prisoner's comfort," Gradlon replied. "And to preemptively answer what will surely be your next question, no one escorted me to my cell. I was dropped into this tunnel like a rat in a maze, and was told to find my way or die trying."

"Then who locked the trap door?" Gradlon surely hadn't locked himself in.

"The door was locked some time after I found the cell. The day had gone from light to dark, then light again, so I assume it was a single day afterward." Gradlon stumbled. Aodhan offered him an arm, but he righted himself on his own. "A guard—one of *my* guards—poked his head up through the door, brought me a water skin and some cheese and bread, then he left and I heard him bolt the door. He was the last person I saw until you lot appeared."

"You haven't gotten any more food in days, then?" I asked, my stomach cramping in memory of my recent captivity.

"I haven't."

Kelsey made her way to Gradlon, and offered him a granola bar from her bag. "It's a bit soggy, but better than nothing," she said.

"Thank you," Gradlon said, as he bowed his head to her. "I won't forget your kindness."

Then the ground fell out from under us.

I coughed myself awake. Again. Gods below, I was sick of regaining consciousness this way.

"What happened?" I croaked.

"It would appear that the tunnel floor collapsed underneath our feet," Gradlon replied. "We've fallen to a lower level." I heard a click, and Kelsey reignited her lighter. Her, Gradlon, and I were in another dirt tunnel, and the rest were nowhere to be found.

"Da," I yelled. "Aodhan!"

"Kevin," Kelsey screamed.

No responses, not even a whisper.

"We may be quite far down," Gradlon said. "These tunnels are ancient, and riddled with hidden rooms."

"Why didn't you tell us that before?" I snapped.

"Apologies, my lady. When you burst into my cell, I simply didn't think to give you a full lesson on Ker Ys's structural history," he snapped back.

"Sorry," I said. "I'm having a rather bad day. I shouldn't take it out on you."

"I'm going to have a look down the tunnel," Kelsey declared.

"Don't go too far," I said, then she and our only light were gone. As she left the chamber, her lighter had momentarily illuminated Gradlon. He looked gaunt, and far more frail than I'd noticed when we were in his cell.

"You should have that granola," I said.

"Perhaps I should save it," he began, but I shook my head.

"One thing I learned when I was a captive was to not conserve food or water," I said. "Eat it when you have it, because you don't know when you'll get more. When I was in the caves, they starved me for days."

"Wise words," Gradlon said, then I heard the rustle of the wrapper as he tore it open. "Nahel went through all the trouble of capturing you, and then he refused to feed you?"

"He thought if he withheld food from me, my ensuing hunger would make me want to marry him. He was wrong."

"I imagine he was. Nahel is under the impression that since he's a prince, women will fall into his bed with little to no coaxing on his part. He's somewhat correct, but the sort of women he attracts aren't the ones he wants. And the sort of woman he wants tends to not want to have anything to do with him."

I heartily agreed with that. "My mother said that your children are descended from Ran. I imagine that's why she's here now, breaking ships and such."

"Yes. That's true. Ran is their grandmother."

"How did you meet their mother?"

"Ah. Hefring." Gradlon chewed for a moment before he continued. "She was such a beauty, with her eggshell smooth skin, and long silken hair. It seemed to move of its own accord, and she would wrap it around—"

"We don't need those sorts of details," Kelsey said, as she reentered the room. "The tunnel goes on a ways. Might as well stick together and try to find our way out. You can both walk?"

We affirmed that we could, and after we'd sorted ourselves out, we began following Kelsey down the tunnel. "Why are there so many tunnels down here?" I asked. "Is there a cave system, like the one beneath Kilstiffen?"

"These are old mining shafts," Gradlon replied, and I remembered the vast stores of salt that had been Ker Ys's primary trade good. Until I stole it all, that is.

"Was me taking the salt the reason why Corentin put this plan in motion?" I asked.

"You may have forced him to act earlier than he'd planned, but turning Ker Ys into a new Atlantis has been his priority for some time," he replied. "Why do you think I tried for so long to marry him off? But nothing came of that, as you know."

"Is that why you tried to pair Kevin and me with your children?" I pressed. "To speed up New Atlantis?"

"That was a matter of mere survival," Gradlon said. "Ever since my children were born, and those of the Northern Reaches turned against us, we've not done well. My hope was that your dowry would bring some much needed funds into our treasury."

"Then why didn't you try marrying one of Steinar's children?" Kelsey asked. "Too hung up on Hefring?"

"I should have arranged myself a marriage with an heir from one of the other sea kingdoms, but after I met Hefring, I could think of no one else. She and I were a chance meeting," Gradlon added. "I hadn't even known she was with child, not until Ran brought the twins here."

"Hefring didn't bring them herself?"

"She did not," Gradlon said bitterly. "When her parents learned of our relationship, dedicated to each other though we were, they weren't pleased. I had no idea the lengths they would go to in order to keep us apart."

"My mother said the Norse influenced others not to deal with you, but that makes no sense," I said. "Why did they act in a way that also hurt Dahut and Nahel?"

"Simple," Kelsey said. "He hasn't told us the whole story. Something else happened."

Gradlon sighed. "Yes. Something did, though to this day I have no idea what."

"Is this 'something' why you're hiding everything of value in the walls?" I asked. "Which is quite odd, by the way."

"That was to keep Corentin from selling what remained of our heritage to fund his mad plans," Gradlon replied. "Believe me, it was a last resort."

"Speaking of walls, we've come to another one," Kelsey announced. "Or maybe it's a boarded up doorway?"

I approached the wall, and saw the wooden planks that were nailed across the tunnel and barring our way forward. "What's on the other side?" I asked Gradlon.

"Most likely more of the same. Unless..." He approached the planks, and peered through a crack. "We're at the far side of the palace. This is our way out."

"How do we get past?" I felt the planks, and swore when I caught a splinter. "Is there a knob, or handle?"

"This entrance was boarded up some years ago," Gradlon said. "We need to break through the planks."

"We can burn then," Kelsey the arsonist declared, as she held the lighter's flame to the wood. While she willed the tiny flame to catch, I hummed.

I hummed, and my throat didn't hurt.

"*Flames,*" I sang in a croaking voice worthy of Kevin. "*Flames, fire, catch and burn. Grab the wood and watch it churn.*"

"It worked," Kelsey said, as the flames licked up the planks and reduced them to ash. "Meri, your voice is back!"

"Excellent rhyming," Gradlon deadpanned, as we retreated down the tunnel to avoid the fire. "The third line can end in berm. Or turn, perhaps?"

"Feel free to compose the next song," I said. The planks were suddenly engulfed, and I worried the fire would spread back into the tunnel. My fears were unfounded, and the fire died as quickly as it had come to life. As soon as the smoke dissipated, we picked our way over the glowing embers and onto a beach not unlike the one the Camargue had originally deposited us on.

"Are we sure this is the other side of the island?" I asked, then Kelsey pointed toward the sea.

"Meri, look!"

I followed her gaze and saw Ran's massive form standing in the water. She was amazingly tall, and the waves only reached her waist. Her net was slung across her shoulder, and she stalked among the remains of the fleet that bobbed among the breakers.

"What is she looking for?" I asked.

"Anyone still living," Gradlon said. "She'll want to catch them in her net."

"Don't you know her?" I demanded, as I rounded on him. "Can you make her stop?"

"Yes, I am known to Ran, and no, I cannot compel her to do anything," he replied. "Except, perhaps, finally kill me."

I made a wordless sound of frustration, which hurt my semi-healed throat and accomplished exactly nothing. "How do we know who she's already dragged down? And how do we get them back?"

"Meri," Kelsey said, as she grabbed my arm. "I don't see any sailors. I also don't see any bodies."

Gradlon sighed. "That's because Ran will have dragged them all to her lair at the bottom of the sea."

I stared at Gradlon, then I turned my gaze toward the sea. The beach was littered with the remains of ships from Kilstiffen and Ker Ys alike. Out past the breakers, I recognized the mast from one of Evonium's ships. But Kelsey was right. There wasn't a single body among the wreckage, living or otherwise.

"What will Ran do to them?" I demanded.

"Whatever she wants," Gradlon replied. "The ocean floor is Ran's domain."

"My mother is down there!"

"As is my brother, and my son," Gradlon replied. "They may be fools, but they're my fools. I've always forgiven them everything. I'll forgive them their treason, as well. But going up against Ran..." Gradlon shook his head. "No one can defeat her."

"Meri can," Kelsey said. "Now that Meri's got her voice back, she can do anything."

"I can," I said; then, more definitively, "I can. I defeated Donn, and an ankou, and a host of other creatures..." Ran picked that moment to roar, and strike terror into my very soul. For all my past victories, I'd never faced a creature as powerful as her.

I tamped down my fear, and continued, "Everything can be defeated, but I'll need your help. Does Ran have a weakness?"

"Gold," Gradlon replied. "Ran loves gold, more so than her children or even her husband. Dazzle her with gold, and you might distract her long enough to escape."

"Gold," I repeated. "I can manage that."

"But how will you manage getting to the ocean floor?" Kelsey asked. "You don't swim. Can you sing your way down?"

Instead of replying, I stared at the sea, and the rather gaping hole in my plan. Even though I was half merrow by birth, I'd never felt drawn to the sea, not like Aodhan or even my da had always been. On the few occasions I had gotten into the ocean, it had been accidental, and I had not enjoyed it. I recalled when the sea had snatched me off Aodhan's boat, how the cold water that had pressed against my skin and made my lungs feel like they were about to burst, and shuddered. Before I could give voice to any of that, Kelsey pointed toward the shore.

"Are those survivors?" Kelsey asked.

"Ran doesn't leave survivors," Gradlon said, but I was already jogging toward the water. What had initially looked like people swimming up to the beach turned out to be a pod of seals. Behind me, Gradlon muttered that I'd lost my mind, but I ignored him. Heart in my throat, I ran to the water's edge, hoping beyond hope I knew who was under those skins.

The lead seal flopped into the shallows and waved her flippers at me. I dropped to my knees in the surf as the creature stood up, and Rose Fennimore, my music teacher and the leader of County Clare's pod of selkies, unzipped her sealskin cloak.

"Rose," I said, happy and amazed and so, so grateful she was there. "What are you doing here, of all places? And how did you all get past Ran?"

"That one takes no notice of those she deems beneath her," Rose said, as she tossed a glance over her shoulder toward the sea goddess. "As for why we're here, Lorcan stopped by our beach and mentioned you could use some reinforcements for this mad venture of yours."

"He was right," I said. "Rose, Kilstiffen's navy has been devastated and Ran's trapped nearly everyone at the bottom of the ocean."

"You're needing a way down to the sea floor, then," Rose said. "We can help with that. What about those two?" she asked, with a nod toward Kelsey and Gradlon. "Hello, Kelsey."

"Hi," Kelsey said, with a wave.

"This is Gradlon, the king of Ker Ys," I said. "His brother and son are down with the rest. If you help to rescue them, Ker Ys will owe you."

"Big time," Kelsey added.

"Fine," Gradlon said. "Return my family to me, and my meager kingdom will be yours for the asking. And if you find my Hefring somewhere in Ran's hall, tell her I love her still."

Rose stilled. "Hefring? Ran's third daughter? I'm sorry to tell you this, but she passed some time ago."

Gradlon stumbled, and Kelsey steadied him. "How do you know this?" he asked.

"We who live in the sea hear all the news," Rose replied. "Hefring was a mere slip of a thing, always had been. That had never been an issue until she found herself heavy with twins. She didn't survive their birth."

"Oh," I said, as I covered my mouth with my hand. Ran's vendetta against Ker Ys suddenly made sense; Gradlon had gotten Hefring pregnant, and in Ran's mind, caused her death.

"I had no idea," Gradlon mumbled. "All this time, I thought she merely didn't want to see me..." He straightened, and said to Rose,

"Thank you, for telling me. Bring my son back alive, and my kingdom is yours."

"I appreciate the offer, but I'll be more than happy with just your gratitude," Rose replied. "Meri, let's get you below."

"All right," I said, not relishing the thought of being underwater again. I turned to Kelsey, and said, "While I'm down there, find Da and Aodhan and Kevin. Once you're all together, figure out what kind of an offense you can still muster. I've a feeling this isn't over, not by a long shot."

Kelsey nodded. "I'll find them. We'll make a rock solid plan, too."

"I know you will." I faced Gradlon. "I'm so sorry about Hefring. I'll find Nahel for you."

Gradlon nodded. "Thank you, my dear. He's a foolish child, but he's mine. He's almost all I have left of my Hefring."

"We'll find Dahut, too," I said, though I didn't relish the thought of facing her or the Camargue again. I didn't mention Corentin, since I had no idea what I would do if confronted with him, except perhaps spit in his face. Leaving those problems for another time, I took Rose's hand.

"I'm ready."

THE LAIR OF THE SEA GODDESS

As it turns out, seals can swim especially fast.

Rose remained in her human form and looped her arm with mine as we waded into the water. Once we were out far enough, we plunged into the icy waves, and the rest of the pod formed a protective barrier around us as we sped toward the sea floor. After what seemed like the barest second, we were stepping into an air-filled structure on the ocean's bottom.

"I'm so happy to breathe," I said, as I gulped the humid air.

"As am I," Rose said. "Now, let's have a look around."

She made a clicking noise in the back of her throat, and the rest of the pod stepped out of their skins and began skulking about the place. On closer inspection, we saw that the walls were made of old bleached coral, though the floor was cold, wet sand. Water dripped from where the walls joined the ceiling, and clumps of seaweed and driftwood littered the ground. The whole edifice seemed like it had been hastily cobbled together and plunked into the water near Ker Ys.

That meant Ran had fully anticipated taking prisoners.

"Odd place for a sea goddess to set up," I muttered.

A man's voice asked, "Were you expecting marble floors and a golden roof?"

I looked toward the voice, and saw Oscar step out of the shadows.

"You're all right," I gasped.

"I'm in one piece," he said, then he spied Rose. "My selkie songstress," he said, as he spread his arms wide.

"Hello, you." Rose approached Oscar and embraced him, then she stood on her toes and kissed my uncle on the mouth. Interesting.

"Where are the rest of our people?" I asked. "Wandering about like you are?"

"If only," Oscar replied. "Almost everyone who was caught in Ran's net is in the central chamber. They're alive, for now."

"How did you avoid being captured?" I asked.

"Everyone knows that Oscar's far too slippery for a net," Rose said.

"My feathered spy warned me that Ran was about to strike," Oscar began, referencing the grey bird he'd created with his harp. "I readied myself to swim to shore, but then I saw my sisters getting dragged down in Ran's net, so I jumped in after them. It was no fun plunging into the sea while hoping to find an air pocket, I'll tell you that."

"Brave and foolish in equal measures, same as ever," Rose said, and Oscar grinned. Watching my uncle and my music teacher flirt at the bottom of the sea was a strange feeling.

"You said almost everyone is in the center of this place?" I asked, mostly to get them to stop making eyes at each other. "Who isn't?"

Oscar's face darkened. "Ran's taken an interest in the king."

"Is Grandfather all right?" I asked.

"Unsure. She's got Corentin with her, as well. Seems she's a taste for rulers."

"Corentin's no ruler," I said. "We found Gradlon stuck in a dungeon behind a dining room. Dahut lied when she claimed he was dead."

"We can work with that information," Oscar said. "What's the plan?"

"My sole objective was to get down here and find out who was still alive," I said. "As for getting them out, according to Gradlon, Ran gets distracted by gold."

"More information we can use," Oscar said with a grin. "Meri, at this rate, you'll be the queen of the hellions. Come with me. I'll bring you to where the bulk of the captives are."

Rose made some more of those clicking noises in the back of her throat, then we followed Oscar down the coral hallway. "What did you tell the pod?" I asked.

"I told them we're going further in, and that we're with Oscar," she began, then a few clicks came in reply. "They want me to be careful with him. We've had a few adventures together, you see."

I almost asked what sort of adventures, then I remembered their kiss. "Will the rest keep a lookout?"

"They will, and they can also help bring people to the surface quickly and quietly. Don't worry, Meri. This Ran's but one person. Together, we can handle her."

"Last I saw, she was a rather large, scary person," I said.

"True, but we've both faced our share of monsters. We'll put this one behind us soon enough."

"I hope you're right." I stared at Oscar's back as we followed him through Ran's makeshift prison. His harp remained snug in its case, which was a good sign. Perhaps with my singing and his playing we could raise this place to the surface much like we'd raised Kilstiffen.

The hallway led to a large room cordoned off with tall, curved posts set into the sand. "Is this another type of coral?" I asked, as I gingerly touched the off-white pillars.

"That's not coral. The fence is made up of whale rib bones," Oscar replied. "There's whole cities built from dead creatures down here."

"Barbarous," Rose hissed. "To live inside a creature's corpse is an abomination."

"On that, love, we do agree." Oscar leaned against a rib, and pushed it with his full body weight. "Give me a musical hand, Meri?"

I sang a few light notes intended to reduce the bone's weight. Oscar's voice joined mine, and a moment later, he pulled the rib out of the sand and heaved it to the side. "This opening ought to be wide enough to get everyone through. Everyone except Fionn, that is," he said, as moved through the bones sideways. "No idea what Scáthach's been feeding that giant. Onward now, ladies."

Rose and I slithered through the rib bones, and we made our way deeper into Ran's lair. The floor sloped downward, as if a pit had been dug into the ocean floor. Many other bones, these sawn off and pointed like massive teeth, were shoved into the sand and angled downward, I assumed to hinder any escape attempts. Down past the teeth and at the lowest point in the room, I saw people clustered together.

"Is that everyone, except Grandfather and Corentin?" I asked.

"Near as I can tell, yeah." Oscar glanced at Rose. "I was thinking about flooding the place so everyone could swim out, but I'm not sure how sound the walls are. They could collapse inward and crush everyone."

"We also don't know how many are injured, and lack the strength to swim," Rose added. "Let's get closer, and have a look at what we're dealing with."

"It gets steep from here on in," Oscar warned us, then we began picking our way down the sandy incline. Once we were closer to the captives I saw rows of amazingly large open shark mandibles—each of them lined with pointed teeth—suspended over the prisoners.

"What sort of beast are those from?" I asked. A man could easily stand up inside those jaws.

"Sharks get awful big down here," Rose replied. "I assume those are rigged to fall on anyone trying to make a break for it?"

"Aye," Oscar said, then he pointed to the left. Some of those jaws had gotten loose and fallen down to the sand. A few had bodies pinned underneath. "Seems to be a good deterrent."

"What triggers them to fall?" Rose asked.

"I'll investigate that," Oscar said, as he moved off to the left. I took a step toward the fallen jaws, and paused when I saw blonde hair on one of the bodies. Swallowing the lump in my throat, I moved closer, then I stopped. Those few likely were beyond anything I could do, at least for the moment. I needed to concentrate on helping the living before I could spend time mourning the dead.

I turned on my heel and moved toward the prisoners, scanning the crowd for a glimpse of my mother. Instead, my gaze fell on a red-haired woman who was sitting up against a boulder, her head lolled to the side and her legs stretched out in front of her. As I got closer, I realized her hair wasn't red, but blonde that had been stained by blood from a rather nasty head wound. Then I saw her bracelets, two golden cuffs with an iridescent fish scale pattern.

"Mama," I called, as I broke into a run. Fionn stepped out from behind the boulder and held out his arm.

"Stop," he bellowed. My arms windmilled as I skidded to a halt. "The perimeter's warded," Fionn continued. "One wrong step and the shark teeth will start falling again."

"Is the entire border spelled?" I asked.

"The current assumption is yes." Fionn crouched down and checked the woman's pulse points, and I realized that he was caring for Scáthach, not my mother. "Everyone who's tried to run off has been hit."

"All right, we'll assume it's all spelled." I was standing about two metres from Fionn, though most of the rest were farther away in the centre of the depression. Rose caught up to me, and gasped at the sight of Scáthach's wound. "Did one of those jaws fall onto Scáthach?"

"No. She was wounded in the battle," he replied. "When Ran whipped her net onto one of the ships, the hull splintered and boards went flying. One of them struck Scáthach, got her right in the head. I saw it happen."

"Was that when you jumped overboard?"

"Aye." Having finished checking over Scáthach, he arranged her braid against her shoulder before caressing her cheek. "But don't you worry about my Shadow. She's a strong one. As soon as she wakes, we'll fight our way out of here, back to back like we always do." Fionn squeezed Scáthach's hand, then he stood and faced me. "Who'd you come down with?"

"Oscar, and Rose's pod of selkies," I craned my neck to see around him. "Is my mother near?"

"Aye," he said, then he turned and cupped his hand to his mouth. "Aoife!"

"Is it Scáthach?" Mama demanded, as she burst forth from the throng a moment later. When she saw me, she sagged in relief. "Meri! Where are the boys?"

"Up top with Kelsey. Get this, Gradlon's alive."

Mama swore. "I should have demanded Corentin's head all those years ago. That fool and his vendetta are destroying everything he touches."

"This lie might be Dahut's," I said. "Also, I promised Gradlon I would get Nahel out of here."

"They we'll do so," Mama said. "Do we have a plan?"

"I planned on securing some gold, and using it to distract Ran while the selkies help the rest escape," I replied. "That's all I have."

"That's a good start," Mama said, then she saw her brother. "Oscar!"

"No time for joy at my arrival," Oscar said, as he jogged toward us. "I've just finished walking the perimeter. The spelled object—that which is keeping the jaws aloft—is a sea serpent's skeleton. The tail is crammed right into the mouth like a true ouroboros."

"Can we break it apart, make an escape route?" I asked.

Oscar shook his head. "Not likely. These sorts of serpents have bones like iron, which is why they make such good spear tips. However, I do have an idea. Since we managed to raise Kilstiffen earlier, I propose we sing to raise the skeleton out of the sand and hold it a meter or so aloft. You see, I believe that what triggers the teeth to fall is when a certain amount of weight is on top of the skeleton."

"And with it aloft, everyone can escape underneath the bones," I said. "All right, let's do it."

"There is a wrinkle," Oscar said. "The serpent's skull is massive, and weighs as much as a mountain. I'm not sure we can raise it, and I'm also not sure this will work unless the entire skeleton is aloft."

"If we can raise Kilstiffen we can raise a bloody skull," I said.

"I'll hold up the skull," Fionn said. "You lot take care of the spine, and I'll keep the skull aloft for as long as necessary."

"Fionn," Mama began, but he made a cutting motion with his hand.

"Aoife, you know I'm the strongest one here," he said. "Just promise me you'll get my Shadow out if anything happens to me."

"We're not going to let anything happen to you, and you know we will see to both you and Scáthach," Mama said. "Thank you, Fionn."

"Just doing what I was born to do," he said. "Now, Rose, where are the rest of the selkies that arrived with you?"

BENEATH THE SERPENT'S SKULL

After Rose's pod joined us, our next task was locating the serpent's skeleton and marking the edges of where the bones lay beneath the sand. Oscar was right, it was enormous. I hoped Fionn hadn't been exaggerating when he claimed to be the strongest one here.

Our plan was simple enough. Merrows were stationed around the perimeter, and, much like when we raised Kilstiffen, we would sing in unison with the objective of raising the serpent. We would start with the head; once it was aloft, Fionn would plant himself underneath, then the rest of us would handle raising the spine and ribs. When the skeleton was high enough, we would begin the retreat, and the selkies would help lead everyone to the surface.

And once the evacuation was underway, Mama and I would track down Ran and rescue the king.

"You're going to have to get Corentin, too," Rose said, as we made the final preparations to raise the serpent. "If for no other reason than to make sure he's properly punished."

"Leaving him down here would be an excellent punishment." I stretched my neck from side to side, and watched as my mother and Oscar returned to us. Nahel was nowhere to be found, and despite my promise to Gradlon I wasn't too concerned about him. Surely Ran would see her grandson to safety.

As for Mama and Oscar, they had meticulously mapped out where the serpent's skull lay beneath the sand, so Fionn could get himself underneath the behemoth as soon as possible. On the one hand, I wondered how heavy this skull could possibly be. On the other, would Fionn's strength be enough?

"We've done all we can," Oscar said, as he withdrew his harp. "Rose, is your pod ready to start the evacuation?"

"We are," she replied. The selkies were arranged at equidistant points around the perimeter, ready to ferry the wounded and lead the rest up to Ker Ys. "Bring me Scáthach first. I'll get her to the surface, and then come back for the rest."

"Thank you," Fionn said, as he lifted Scáthach in his arms. He held her for a moment, his forehead pressed against hers, then he passed her to my mother.

"Take her spear," Fionn said, as he tossed the weapon onto the sand near my feet. "Might give you an edge against Ran."

Mama nodded, then she looked at Oscar. "Let's begin."

"Let's." Oscar withdrew his harp, and strummed a few notes. Rose and I matched the tune, then one by one the merrows and selkies took up the song. The ground quaked and swayed beneath us, then a wide crack appeared in the sand. Seconds later, I saw the top of the skull. With a mighty shudder, it began to rise.

And rise.

Oscar was right. The serpent's skull was enormous, easily as big as a cottage. What's more, its bones weren't the same pale grey as the whale bone bars that circled around us. The serpent's skeleton was the color of charcoal, as if we'd dragged it out of hell's hottest fire instead of the ocean's floor.

At last the skull was fully aloft. Fionn strode underneath the blackened bone and planted himself below the rear curve, using his shoulders and back to take the brunt of the weight. "Now, Aoife," he bellowed.

Quick as lighting, Mama darted under the skull, and passed my aunt to Rose. As Rose and others fled toward the surface, Mama unbuckled her leather breastplate.

"What are you doing?" I asked.

"You said gold distracts Ran," she replied, then she pulled off the breastplate and revealed the gold chain mail shirt she wore beneath. She was the only one with the right to wear golden mail, because she was the champion of Kilstiffen.

"As you can see, I'm positively dripping in gold," she continued, then she hefted Scáthach's spear. "Let's go get the king, aye?"

"Less talking, more going," Oscar said. "It won't be long before Ran knows what we're up to."

I nodded. "Let's move. Stay strong, Fionn!"

"Worry not, Meri," Fionn ground out. "Weighs less than a kitten."

Mama put her hand on my shoulder, and we left the evacuation in search of Ran. The inner corridors were a maze of bleached coral walls and gloppy sand pits, and we were soon lost. After a few minutes of this, we reached a point where the corridor went in two directions. My mother took a deep breath, and sang.

A moment later, an answering note drifted toward us from the left.

"That's Papa," she said, and we sprinted down the left hand corridor. It let out into a vast area walled not with coral, but the ocean itself.

"What is holding back the water?" I wondered aloud.

"Worry about that later," Mama said, then she pointed toward the far side of the chamber. "There he is!"

Across the watery chamber were my grandfather and Corentin. They were alive, and at first glance, appeared unharmed. Both of them were secured to yet another whale bone with lengths of rope.

"Aoife," Grandfather said, relief colouring his voice. "And Meri!"

"Hello, Aoife," Corentin said. Mama glared at him. He turned to me, and opened his mouth.

"Don't you dare speak to me," I said, then I asked Grandfather, "Are you all right?"

"As well as can be. Where are the rest?"

"Getting up to the surface." Mama scrutinized the ropes around Grandfather's torso. "You can't sing the ropes apart?"

"No," he replied. "The ropes are immune to my magic."

"Then what are we to do," I began, since we all had the same type of abilities. That was when Ran, who clearly cared more about her captive kings than the rest of her prisoners, crashed through the wall of water and roared.

"Use the spear on the ropes," Mama said, as she thrust the weapon at me. "I'll handle Ran!"

"A lot has happened," I said, as I sawed at the ropes near Grandfather's elbow. "Gradlon's not dead, for one. For two, Dahut and the Camargue are what really sank the fleet. There's some kind of half-baked revenge plot going on here."

"Not revenge," Corentin said. "We mean to return Ker Ys to its former glory!"

"You are equally lame in all aspects of life, aren't you?" I said, as the ropes fell apart. Mama was right to leave me the spear. It cut through the ropes like a hot knife through butter. "Also, Grandfather, when I was being held down in the council's caves, Corentin beat me within an inch of my life."

"Did he." Grandfather shrugged himself free of the ropes, then he grabbed Corentin's chin and squeezed. "Explain why I shouldn't kill you."

"I can help you defeat Ran," he blubbered.

Grandfather glanced toward my mother. She was fearlessly harrying the sea goddess with a jagged length of coral. "Aoife seems to be handling that on her own. Yet again, you've proven yourself to be useless. Meri, what should we do with him?"

"Let's leave him here with Ran," I said as I sliced Corentin's ropes apart. Grandfather let up on his grip, and Corentin fell to his knees. "I'm sure she'll think of something painful and humiliating to do with him."

A scream tore the air, then my mother was flung onto the sand at our feet. Ran strode up to us, and bared her teeth. "Yes," she growled. "I've plans for each one of you."

FRAGARACH

I lunged toward my mother, but Grandfather clamped his hand down on my shoulder. "Stay with me, Meri," he said. "Aoife can handle herself in battle."

"Can she?" I asked. Mama still hadn't gotten up, though she was moving and therefore alive, and Ran loomed over her like a watery demon. Suddenly Mama braced her arms behind her head, then she leapt upward and delivered an uppercut to Ran's jaw. The sea goddess stumbled backward as Mama drew her sword.

"I don't know what you're after, Ran, but you'll not harm my family to get it," Mama said. "We've done nothing to you!"

"You're allied with murders," Ran seethed. "Ker Ys is a land of killers!"

"She's upset over Hefring," I yelled. "Her daughter died in childbirth having the twins."

"To be separated from your child is the worst pain imaginable," Mama said, then she widened her stance and levelled her sword at Ran's throat. "And that is why I refuse to let you harm my own daughter."

"Why is she so angry now?" Grandfather asked. "Hefring bore the twins over twenty years ago. Something else is at play." He glanced at Corentin. "What have you done?"

"Ran is against our alliance with the council," Corentin replied. "She believes that establishing a New Atlantis on Ker Ys will erase her daughter's legacy."

"That can't be all of it," I said. "When I was in the cave, I heard you say you needed me and my brother for your plan to work. What were you going to do with us?"

"Yes, Corentin," Grandfather said, as he took a step toward the coward. "What were your plans for my grandchildren?" Corentin shrank back from my grandfather, and held up his arm to shield himself. Before Grandfather could press Corentin further, Nahel approached us.

"He promised us we would have our marriages, and that we would rule," Nahel said. "We were going to use Kilstiffen's treasury to conquer all the sea kingdoms in the Atlantic, and make New Atlantis the most powerful monarchy in history." He looked toward his grandmother. "Ran did not agree with our plans."

"Stay back," I hissed. I'd seen Nahel use his wave dancer abilities more than once, and we were surrounded by water. To my grandfather, I said, "We need to neutralize his powers."

"You already have." Nahel withdrew the green stone Aodhan had flung onto his back. "I'm not sure what this stone is, but it took away all of my abilities."

I blinked. "Forever?"

"I don't know." He tossed the stone at me. "Now I have no power over water, no kingdom, and no wife. I'm nothing now."

I caught the stone, and shoved it into my pocket. "You never had me."

"But you've lost us the rest," Corentin hissed at Nahel. "Stop giving the enemy weapons, you traitor!"

"You are the traitor," Grandfather bellowed. "The sea kingdoms have an accord, one that has stood for thousands of years. Who do you think you are to break it?"

"He's not even a king," I added. "As long as Gradlon lives, Corentin has no say in what Ker Ys does."

Ran lowered her net. "Gradlon lives?"

"Yes," I said. "These two idiots imprisoned him, and went off on this mad plan." I glanced at Nahel. "Your father is alive."

"But my mother is not," he said, as his head drooped. "I always thought she was waiting for me somewhere in the Northern Reaches." For the barest second, I empathized with Nahel, then I remembered how he withheld food from me and threated to force me into his bed.

"Where do we stand, Ran?" Mama asked. She hadn't lowered her sword or relaxed her pose, even though Ran had turned her attention elsewhere. "This all seems to be something of a misunderstanding, and the villain is right there. Are we good?"

Ran tossed her net over her shoulder and scrutinized Corentin. "How do we know these statements aren't more lies?"

"Simple." Mama sheathed her sword, then drew the second blade she kept strapped to her back. "This is Fragarach," Mama explained. "Anyone at held at the blade's point is compelled to answer any question, completely and truthfully." She strode up to Corentin, and poked the sword's tip against his throat.

"Watch it," Corentin growled.

"No." My mother moved the blade ever so slightly, leaving a trail of red against his skin. "What were your plans for my children?"

"Ransom." Corentin's eyes widened, as if he was shocked at how easily the truth fell from his lips. "We would force the marriage between Nahel and Meri, with the hope Kevin would then agree to wed Dahut. Afterward, we would ransom them to Steinar. Once the ransom plot was complete, we would rebuild our fleet and invade Kilstiffen with the goal of emptying the treasury."

"I would rip out your heart before I sent you one copper coin," Grandfather said. "I shall enjoy discussing your punishment with Gradlon."

Mama glanced at the king, then she flipped Fragarach around and pointed it at Nahel's heart. "Your intent was to *force* a marriage?" she demanded.

"If need be, yes," Nahel replied. "Meri was promised to me, and don't start with 'Manannán voided the betrothal' because I don't care. As far as I'm concerned, she's mine."

Moving faster than my eyes could track, Mama darted behind Nahel and grabbed him by the hair while her blade's edge pressed against his throat. "Touch my daughter in any way and I will kill you so slowly, you'll be an elder before you finally pass," she hissed.

"I didn't touch her." Nahel's wild eyes beseeched me for help. "Meri, tell her!"

"It's true," I said. "He didn't lay a finger on me. He just starved me for six days while he tormented me with tales of his desires for the bedchamber."

Mama twisted her hand in Nahel's hair, then she flung him at Ran's feet. "The boy needs to learn manners," my mother said. "Perhaps you should instill some in him."

"I agree," Ran said. "He's spent too much time among the barbarians of Ker Ys. Perhaps time spent among his mother's people will remedy his bad choices."

"I did promise Gradlon that I would bring him back," I said, not that I cared about what happened to Nahel. However, I was loathe to break my word.

"Fear not, merrow," Ran said. "I'll bring him up to his father, and after they say their farewells, we'll be off to my household."

"What about this one?" Mama asked, as she poked Corentin's arm with her sword.

"We shall punish him, along with the rest of the council," Grandfather said, then he turned to the sea goddess and bowed. "Until we meet again, Ran."

"Until then, Steinar," Ran said, then she grabbed Nahel's shoulder, and they melted into the wall of water. Mama wrestled Corentin to his feet and shoved him forward.

"Walk," she ordered. "My blade's a hair's breadth from your back, so keep a brisk pace."

"After all that, we're just parting ways?" I asked. "Ran destroyed three fleets over this 'misunderstanding'!"

"What would you have me do, Meri?" Grandfather asked. "Send her a bill?" When I didn't reply, he said, "Our reparations will come. When Ran favors someone or some place, she will gift them with calm seas, bountiful harvests, and good weather."

"I suppose that's her currency," I said, and he nodded. "What about the council?"

"They will be dealt with, along with this traitor," he replied. "Perhaps we should just leave them in a room with your mother for a time."

"An excellent idea," Mama said. "After I chop the balls off this one, I'll shove them down the councilors' throats."

"What do my balls have to do with any of this?" Corentin demanded.

"Keep it up and they'll have nothing to do with anything." Mama replied, then she nudged his back with the tip of her sword. "Walk faster."

ESCAPE AND CAPTURE

As we ascended through Ran's makeshift lair, the walls and ceiling began coming apart. We dodged the falling chunks of coral and driftwood, and it wasn't long before we met up with those evacuating from the central prison. I could hear the selkies issuing commands in their distinctive calls, and Oscar's harp as he kept the serpent's bones aloft.

"We should check on Oscar," I said. "And Fionn!"

"Rose won't let Oscar be left behind," Mama said. "As for Fionn, he's got to be the last one out. He knew what he was getting into when he volunteered to hold up the skull."

"Don't worry about Oscar and Fionn, Meri," Grandfather said, when I looked back toward the serpent's chamber. "Our family is strong, and we were born to navigate the seas."

I had no choice but to believe them. We fled through the lair, Corentin still prodded along by my mother's sword at his back. We reached the outer walls as the ceiling caved in behind us.

"I can't swim," I said, my voice trembling. Behind us, I could hear the sea rushing in. I didn't know if those in front of us could swim either, and I momentarily feared we would become trapped in Ran's lair. "Grandfather, we're all going to drown."

"We are not," he said, as he tightened his hand on my arm. "Match my voice."

I was a bare second from demanding how one man's song could save us all—then I remembered how he'd single handedly devastated Ker Ys's army with naught but his voice. I placed my hand atop his, and we sang together.

Amazingly, the water held back long enough for everyone to exit the lair, then our combined songs lifted us to the surface. We walked out of the surf along with the rest as if we were on our way to the park, not newly escaped from a prison on the sea floor. As for the beach, it was pure chaos, with people shouting and searching for their friends and comrades. A hand reached out from the throng to help me along. It turned out to be Scáthach.

"All my girls are safe," Grandfather declared, then he glanced toward the water.

"You always tell me to have faith, so now we need to have faith in Oscar," I said. Grandfather nodded, then he faced the waves with his arms crossed over his chest. I half thought he was going to go below and grab Oscar by the scruff of his neck.

"I'm glad you're awake," I said to Scáthach.

"The wound looks worse than it is, I'm sure." Red still matted the hair on the side of Scáthach's head, but her eyes were clear, and her voice was steady. "Where's Fionn?"

"Holding the serpent's skull aloft so we could all escape underneath it," I replied.

A muscle jumped in Scáthach's jaw. "I'll give him another two minutes to get himself up here, then I'm going after him. Is that the bastard prince?" she asked, jerking her chin toward Corentin.

"In the flesh," Mama replied, then she grabbed Corentin's shoulder and shoved him down to the sand. "Kneel," she ordered, then we heard Da calling her name.

"Brian," Mama called out, then she sheathed her sword and ran into his arms.

"My beauty," Da said, as he pressed his face against her hair. "You're all right?"

I didn't hear her answer, since Aodhan picked that moment to sprint toward me. "Meri, Meri, Meri," he said, as he tackled me in a massive embrace. "I am never letting go of you."

"I missed you so much," I said, as I mashed myself against his chest. He drew back and tilted up my chin.

"When Kelsey told us you went under with Rose I almost had a heart attack," he said. "I was so worried about you being down there without me to help you swim."

"I couldn't find you," I said. "But you're okay? What happened after we fell through the bottom of the mine?"

"We found our way out, and met up with Kelsey and Gradlon." He kissed my forehead. "And I'm perfect, now that I've got you."

The selkies began chittering. I moved to the side and saw Rose walking out of the surf carrying an unconscious Oscar across her back. We rushed toward them as Rose flopped onto the sand, and Oscar rolled to the side of her.

"Fool was going to stay down there until the bitter end," she said, then she saw Scáthach. "Fionn was right behind me."

"I'm going after him," Scáthach said. "Aoife, where's my spear?"

A massive dark object ejected from the waves. It was the sea serpent's skull, and it crashed to the beach and skidded to a halt on the far side of the sandbar. It had barely stopped moving when Fionn himself strode out of the surf, wearing a grin and not looking the least bit winded.

"You carried the bloody skull up from the sea floor?" Scáthach demanded.

"I thought we might need it," he said, as he stood in front of Scáthach. "Why? Was that wrong?" She glared at him for another moment, then she fell into his arms.

"Next time, leave it and return to me quicker," she said.

"Aye, love," Fionn said. "Next time, I'll leave all the spoils and hurry back to you."

I tightened my arms around Aodhan, filled with joy not only due to our victory, but all the happy reunions on the beach. "This has turned out rather differently than I expected."

"It did, but it's a good ending nonetheless," he said. "That's Corentin?" he asked, jerking his chin toward the Ker Ysian traitor.

"The coward himself," I replied. "My mother seems to have called dibs on killing him, but she'll probably let you beat him a bit."

"Oh, so we're sharing punishment, now?"

I laughed, then quieted down as Da strode up to Corentin.

"I understand that you've been after my children," Da said, in that genial way of his. Anyone who didn't know him wouldn't realise he was boiling mad. "Exactly why did you think that was a good plan?"

"I don't need to answer to you," Corentin snapped.

"Don't you?" Da glanced at Mama, who approached Corentin and once again leveled Fragarach at his throat. "Seems that it would be in your best interest."

"You let your wife fight your battles?" Corentin demanded.

Da shrugged. "When your wife is Kilstiffen's deadliest warrior, it's usually the best course of action."

"Ask him what he was going to do after he ransomed us," I said. "He said they would ransom Kevin and me and use us to drain the treasury, but he didn't say how."

Mama poked her sword onto Corentin's Adam's apple. "Answer, or I'll gut you like a fish."

Corentin sighed. "Everyone knows that Kilstiffen's royal family is the city's true protection. Many operations within the kingdom can only be completed by a blood relation. Therefore, if Meri and Kevin proved noncompliant we would cut off their hands and pluck out their eyes, and use their unique fingerprints and retinas to access the vaults. Whether or not they cooperated, we would seize the treasury regardless."

I gasped, as Aodhan tightened his arms around me. Before anyone could speak or scream or cut Corentin's bloody head off, Dahut leapt out of the sea.

"So that's how you were going to do it," Dahut said, then she yanked me out of Aodhan's arms and dragged me into the waves.

THE PEARL

What felt like mere seconds after Dahut pulled me off the beach at Ker Ys, she tossed me out of the ocean and onto a different shore. I rolled onto my back as I spluttered and coughed up seawater, and saw a glint of gold out of the corner of my eye. Intrigued, I pushed myself up on my elbows so I could have a better look, then I gasped.

We were on Kilstiffen's shore.

"How did we get here so fast?" I asked. Ker Ys was in the English Channel, and Kilstiffen was a few kilometres off the west coast of Ireland. We'd travelled between the two kingdoms in less than a minute.

"I'm a wave dancer. The water is my domain." Dahut rubbed one of the Camargue's noses. "That was a good trick, no?"

"It felt like I was being pulled through a waterfall." I got to my feet and surveyed the rest of the landscape. Kilstiffen remained above the waves, and the sunlight reflecting off the golden roofs was almost too much to bear. Then I turned around and saw the Irish shore looming in the distance.

"We need to submerge the city," I said. "If it remains above for too long, who knows how the surface world will react."

"Oh, is your home in danger?" Dahut asked. "Are you willing to go to great lengths to keep your way of life safe, and to protect your people?"

I narrowed my eyes at her. "I get it, really I do. And I don't think you're wrong for wanting to protect Ker Ys from the likes of Corentin or even Gradlon."

She blinked. "You don't?"

"Corentin is a lunatic living out his revenge fantasy," I began, then I recalled that he was Dahut's uncle. "Sorry. We can't choose our relatives, can we?"

"You might as well have, Meri," she snapped. "Your family is stacked with gods and kings and legendary heroes. Others would kill to have just one of your magnificent relations."

Her use of the word kill gave me pause. "What do you mean to do here, Dahut?"

"We're going to start by opening the vaults," she began. "But don't worry. Even after I've removed Kilstiffen's gold, I won't let your people starve. I'm not like my uncle or my father."

"Maybe Gradlon gets a bad rap," I said, desperate to stall her. If she could slither through the waves lightning fast, one of the merrows or selkies we'd left behind on Ker Ys must be able to do so as well. Someone—hopefully several someones—must be looking for us even now. "He only just found out what happened to your mother. He's probably going to need you now more than ever."

"He's always needed me," Dahut seethed. "Dahut this, Dahut that. Dahut, your brother can't manage as well as you, can you do this, too?" She grabbed handfuls of her hair and screamed at the clouds.

"And after all that—after everything I did for him—he turned to Nahel and Corentin for help," she continued. "They wanted to destroy everything we had left to become New Atlantis. None of them listened when I told them it was a fool's idea."

"It is a stupid idea," I said. "Even if their mad plan did work, did any of them believe the council would just let it go, and not claim all of Ker Ys for themselves?" I shook my head, as I scanned the horizon. "No. Nothing good would have come of it."

Dahut nodded. "Then you will help me rebuild my city?"

"Um. I guess." I swept my gaze toward the other side of the beach. Still no rescue. "I think it's fair to warn you that I don't actually know how anything works here. I've only been in the palace a few times."

"It's all right, Meri." Dahut extended her hand and offered me a too-wide smile. "I'm quite familiar with how these sorts of cities operate. We can figure it out, together."

"All right." I took a step toward her, but I didn't take her hand. It's one thing to play along with the insane villain, yet another to hold hands with the enemy. Since I wanted to keep her out of the palace for as long as possible, I asked, "Do the Camargue only live near Ker Ys?"

"Yes, they make their home in the marshes on the eastern side of the city," she replied.

"They're amazing," I continued, as I stroked the closest horse's mane. "I've never heard of such horses who could navigate the ocean so well."

"That's all due to your ancestor, Manannán mac Lir," she replied. "They're all descended from his horse, Enbarr."

"Really." I unfastened my pearl pendant, and threaded the chain through the horse's bridle.

"What are you doing?" Dahut demanded.

Ignoring her, I set my hand on the horse's nose. "*Find Manannán, and tell him everything,*" I sang, and all five horses leapt into the waves, hopefully to find Manannán. Their tails were still visible when pain exploded across the back of my head. I fell onto my hands and knees, the sand scraping new injuries on top of the barely healed ones from my time in the caves.

"What have you done," she shrieked. "I need them!"

"I know you do." I touched the back of my head, felt the slick, warm blood flowing out of me. My hand trembled, whether from blood loss or fear I didn't know. "But I need Manannán."

"You don't," she said. "We don't! Damnit, Meri, this is what I've been trying to tell you! We don't need these old, incompetent men in our lives. We are powers in our own right, and we can make our own destiny."

I opened my mouth to sing and show Dahut my power first hand—then I remembered when we faced Donn Dumhach, and Dahut snatched my mother's voice right out of her throat. My voice was still weak from everything I'd put it through over the past few days, and I didn't want to risk losing it altogether.

"All right, Dahut," I said. "How do you propose we begin making our fabulous destiny?"

Dahut grinned, and faced the palace. "For starters, we'll crack that vault. Are all the city's roofs really clad in gold shingles? It's not just golden paint? We should dismantle a few buildings, and find out how much money we're really dealing with."

She went on, detailing how she would strip Kilstiffen down the bare earth to fund her schemes, all while my head swam and blood trickled down my neck. Afraid I would pass out, I braced my hands on my hips, and felt a lump in my pocket. Curious and a bit delirious, I investigated.

It was the green stone Aodhan had used against Nahel.

Slowly, as if I was moving through cold molasses, I got the stone out of my pocket and into my palm. Since being fully upright was out of the question, I struggled onto my knees, and flung the stone at Dahut. It bounced harmlessly off her ankle.

"What was that?" Dahut asked, then green scales formed on her ankle and quickly made their way up her leg.

"What have you done to me?" she screeched, as she tried to wipe away the stone chips that were now covering her.

"The stone was a gift from Sionnan," I said. "Its purpose is to neutralize my enemies."

Stoney green flakes swarmed up and over Dahut's legs and torso as she screamed and screeched. Finally, the green crust closed off her mouth. I wondered if she could breathe under all that. At least she was quiet. I sat heavily on the beach, panting and bleeding and trying to remember everything Oscar had taught me about repairing wounds. I hadn't recalled a single one of his words when a cacophony of voices rang out from the sea. Slowly, I twisted myself around to see what was coming at me now.

The sea serpent's skull was racing across the waves, as fast as a speedboat.

Standing on the skull's nose was Fionn, with Aodhan and my mother scanning the waves on either side of him. "There she is," Aodhan yelled. Fionn steered the skull onto the beach, and it skidded to a halt a few metres from me. Aodhan leapt from the skull and ran to my side.

"She's bleeding," he yelled, then he wrapped his arms around me. "I've got you, Mer. You're going to be just fine."

"You travelled on a skull?" I asked, because wasn't that my most pressing concern?

"We needed to follow you, and there were no ships left. Your grandfather powered it," Aodhan replied, then hands were taking me away from him. I struggled, wondering why Aodhan was letting this happen, then Talia placed her cool hands on my face and head.

"I was so worried about you," I mumbled, as she gently probed my head wound. "My head is broken."

"Don't you worry, love. We'll fix it up good as new," Talia said, then the world went dark.

AND AN AMETHYST

A ray of sunlight found its way onto my face and illuminated the backs of my eyes until everything glowed red. I let myself enjoy the sensation of being awake yet still snuggled in my warm blankets, then my last few moments came back to me.

Ran.

Dahut.

Aodhan's hands covered in my blood...

My eyes snapped open, and the room slowly came into focus. I was in my apartment in Kilstiffen's palace, which made the sunlight both annoying and unusual.

"Aodhan?" I mumbled. He appeared from wherever he'd been, and sat next to me.

"Good morning, beautiful," Aodhan said, as he smoothed my hair back from my face. "How do you feel?"

"Thirsty. Remarkably not sore. And a bit blinded," I added, as I held up my hand to shield my eyes from the bright light. "I didn't even know this room had windows."

"Neither did I, but they're amazing." He stood, and held out his hand. "Up for a bit of exploring?" When I hesitated, he continued, "Just in the room. Promise. Oh, and Talia healed every injury you had, so you should be okay to walk around."

"Really?" I pulled back the bedclothes, and saw smooth, unmarred skin on my legs and hands. I also learned that I was wearing a pink nightgown I had never seen before. "Who put a frilly pink dress on me?"

"Talia picked it out, and I decided not to argue with her. There's a robe right here." He pointed to a cream coloured velvet robe tossed across the foot of the bed, which was an infinitely better option than the pink nightie I was currently wrapped in. Aodhan held it up as I slid my arms into it, then he led me to a bank of windows.

"When we were here before, this wall was covered in a tapestry," he said. "I didn't think much of it at the time, just thought that was how palaces were decorated. But it turns out that when the city's aloft, all the tapestries get pulled back so everyone can enjoy the view."

The windows themselves were gorgeous. Each of them was arched with a central peak, and they were deeply set into the carved stone openings. There were niches carved on the interiors, probably to hold candles and lamps at night. Then I looked out of the window and gasped.

All of Kilstiffen was stretched out before me. The outer walls and structures of the palace sparkled in rich gold and bright white, while the city beyond was a riot of color thanks to the blooming gardens and rich green lawns. A deep blue river snaked through everything, bringing fresh water to everyone who needed it, regardless of the fact that we were in the middle of the ocean.

As for the ocean beyond the city, it was a glorious deep blue. The sun was dipping toward the horizon, and the sky was painted with rich reds and orange streaks.

"We're standing in the most beautiful spot on earth, eh, Mer?" Aodhan slid his arms around my waist and kissed the spot behind my ear. "With the most beautiful person."

"Surely you're referring to yourself." I turned around and slid my arms around his waist, my cheek pressed right over his heart. Heaven. "Did you really turn the serpent's skull into a boat, or was I hallucinating?"

"We didn't have a lot of options." One of Aodhan's hands cupped the back of my head, while the other went to the small of my back. "All of the ships had been destroyed, and Fionn suggested using the skull. He claimed he could sail anything, and he was right. Steinar and your ma gave us a magical push with their voices. We grabbed Talia at the last second, and hoped we would make it here in time."

"I knew you would come for me." Aodhan would always find me, one way or another. I knew that as surely as I knew my own name. "Only you five came on the skull?"

"Yeah. The skull wasn't big enough for many, and a lot of recovery work is underway at Ker Ys. While you were with Talia, Steinar sent a ship back there to pick up your dad and the rest." He kissed the top of my head. "We rushed here to save you, and we found Dahut covered in those green stone chips like what happened to Nahel. Yet again, you saved yourself."

"Really, it was all Sionnan's doing," I demurred. "She gave you the stone in the first place."

"Still. You put it to good use. Where did the water horses end up?"

"I sent them to Manannán. I was doing my best to stall Dahut and keep her out of the palace, so I asked her about the Camargue. She told me then were descended from Manannán's own horse, so I stuck my pearl pendant on one of their bridles and told them to go home. They all jumped into the sea a moment later."

"My brilliant Meri." We stood together for a few moments, holding each other and watching clouds dance across the sky.

"I suppose we should find my mother." Knowing Mama, she would be a ball of nerves until she saw me with her own eyes, and knew I was safe. I would feel the same about her. "What are the odds that someone put some modern clothing in my closet?"

"Nah, it's probably all the same fancy old timey stuff that was here before," he replied. "And you looked amazing in that dress."

"You were quite handsome in your suit, too." I leaned upward and kissed him. "Let's see what costumes we can wear tonight."

As anticipated, my closet was stocked with the same old fashioned formal wear as it had been the last time we were in Kilstiffen. While I picked out a new dress—a dark blue, which was loads better than the pink nightie Talia had selected for me—Aodhan went across the hall to Kevin's rooms, and borrowed one of his outfits. By the time he returned I was already dressed and combing out my hair.

"And somehow, she became more beautiful," Aodhan said, when he saw me sitting in front of the vanity's mirror. "Do you miss the pearl?"

Trust Aodhan to be concerned over the state of my breast. "Actually, I do. Wearing it was reassuring, almost like having a lucky charm." I glanced at him in the mirror. He was wearing a dark navy suit and ivory shirt. "Our outfits match."

"They do, don't they? Although, these clothes are Kevin's, so I hope Steinar wasn't planning on dressing you two up like twins." We laughed, then we left my rooms and went in search of my mother.

A short walk through the sun-drenched palace led us to the throne room. That space also had a wall of tapestries that had been drawn back to allow full view of the sunset. As for my mother, she was sprawled across Grandfather's throne with her feet dangling over the armrests.

"Are you supposed to be sitting up there?" I asked. Mama saw me and grinned.

"The first time I got in trouble when I was a wee hellion was when I painted the throne with big fat polka dots," Mama said, as she stood and walked towards us. "I thought it needed to be prettier." We met, and she embraced me. "My lamb, saving us all yet again."

"All I did was throw a stone at Dahut." I drew back, since Mama's golden chain mail was biting into my neck and arms. I glanced down and saw tiny circles patterned across my skin. "I take it your breastplate remains at the bottom of the sea?"

Mama shrugged. "I can get another. I see Talia's healing went well."

"She's amazing." While I changed, I checked myself out in the mirror. Every single one of my injuries were gone, even down the smallest cuts and scrapes. "Where is she?"

"Having some tea, with yet another of our visitors." Mama led us toward the noon room, which was adjacent to the throne room and Grandfather's favorite place to eat when his family visited. "Come along, now. I'm sure they'd like to see you."

I glanced at Aodhan. He shrugged, so the two of us followed my mother to the noon room. The first person I saw was Talia, seated at the foot of the table, sipping her tea and smiling and some comment I hadn't heard. Wondering what was so amusing, I looked toward the head of the table, and saw my grandfather and Niamh.

"I didn't know you'd be here," I said, then I stared between Talia and my grandmother. "Now I don't know who to hug first!"

"A pleasant predicament, is it not?" Niamh asked. "But I defer to the one who healed you."

"And I defer to your noble grandmother," Talia said.

"Gods below, you're all so formal," Mama said. "I'm starved. Is there anything left over from supper?"

"Supper?" I asked. "We don't have to wait for everyone to get here so we can eat?"

"Absolutely not," Grandfather said, as he pulled out the chair next to me and indicated that I should sit. "Fionn took one of our fastest ships to Ker Ys to collect the rest of our people, but even with his skills they won't return here until tomorrow."

"He must hate being separated from Scáthach," I said.

"Why do you think he volunteered for the voyage?" Grandfather asked, then he rang a bell. A moment later a servant arrived with a cart and laid out bowls of Grandfather's favorite, clam stew.

"I'm afraid this won't be as good as the stew Meri made for me," Grandfather declared, as he sampled a spoonful. "Still, quite a fine meal it is."

"This is amazing," Aodhan said, then he watched as baskets of rolls were set on the table. "You have bread down here?"

"What did you think we ate?" Talia asked. "Seaweed and sand?"

"Honestly, I always hope for the best and gird my stomach for the worst," Aodhan replied. "If you'd ever had canteen services at our school, you'd understand."

"Ugh, don't remind me about school," I said.

"If you don't want to talk about school, we can discuss our city's current position above the waves, instead," Mama said. "I adore sunlight as much as the next person, but if we don't retreat soon, we'll make the leap from legend smack into fact. I'm not sure that's the best plan of action."

"Agreed," Grandfather said. "After dinner, we'll see about going below. Although, since you sung us above the waves, you'll probably have to sing us back down," he added, with a nod toward me.

"I don't know if I'll be able to do that on my own," I said, recalling the dozens of merrows who'd lent their voices to my song. "Certainly not without the pearl."

"Your necklace is here," Niamh said. "Da's got it on him. He's outside, watching over the horses and that evil girl that attacked you."

"Manannán is here?" I asked.

"Oh, yes," Niamh replied. "As soon as the Camargue appeared in the field behind his home with the pearl, he knew something must have happened to you. We rounded up the horses and came above right away."

"Well, thank you," I said. "Why is he still outside?"

Niamh's face darkened. "He's arguing with Ran about how Dahut should be punished."

We finished our stew, then we went outside to speak with Manannán. He was standing on the shore, watching the Camargue frolic in the waves.

"Da," Niamh called, as we approached the sea god. "Meri's finally awake!"

Manannán mac Lir turned around, and I was once again struck by his immense power. "I am glad to hear it. I only wish I could have assisted you, Meri," he said.

"Actually, you did," I said. "When we sang Kilstiffen aloft it only worked because the pearl amplified my voice. Without it, we might not have succeeded."

"Speaking of the pearl," Manannán began, then he reached into the folds of his cloak and withdrew my pendant. "You'll notice that next to the pearl is an amethyst charm. Now, you will be able to reach me through rock, as well as water."

"Thank you," I said, as I accepted my newly upgraded pendant. "I hope I never need to call on you again, but I'm glad I can."

Manannán bowed his head. "I am always here for you, my child. As for Dahut, I've begrudgingly turned her over to Ran. I wanted to drop her into the deepest pit below Tir na nÓg, but Ran has assured me that she can control her granddaughter. I know of your agreement with Gradlon, and Ran has agreed to let the two of them say goodbye to their father before they head north," he added.

"Thank you again," I said. "I know Gradlon's not the best person, but he loves his children."

"All good men do, Meri," Grandfather said, as he glanced at Mama. "There's hope for Gradlon yet."

"What of Corentin?" Mama asked. "He's the fool that started all of this."

"I leave his fate up to Steinar and Gradlon," Manannán replied. "As for the Atlantean council, I will travel to Ker Ys and personally take custody of them. They disrupted many of my kingdoms, and each of them will be held accountable for their crimes."

"No more council?" Aodhan asked. "That's wonderful!"

"Yes, Aodhan, it will be," Manannán said. "Now, we only need to decide what to do with the Camargue."

"Do we need to do anything with them?" I asked. "I thought they belonged to Ker Ys."

"They are blood bonded to the royal family, but when you sent them to me, you voided that association," Manannán replied. "They're now free unto themselves."

"Perhaps we should leave them this way," Niamh suggested. "Let them remain free, as a reminder to all in Ker Ys and Kilstiffen what a madman's plot almost destroyed."

"A fine idea," Manannán said. "As for Kilstiffen, I will ensure it returns below the sunrise after tomorrow. I want your ships to be able to dock safely, being that they're expecting to arrive at the surface harbor."

"Wait, is there an underwater harbor, too?" I asked.

"I'll give you a tour of it after we return below," Mama promised. "Thank you, Manannán, for everything."

"Yes," I added. "We appreciate your help. Thank you."

He graciously bowed his head. "Aoife and Meri, the pleasure is truly all mine."

THE NEXT ADVENTURE

The remnants of Kilstiffen's navy returned sometime during the night. I was alerted to their arrival when Kevin and Kelsey started banging on my and Aodhan's door in the dead of night. After we got dressed the four of us had a small, only slightly teary reunion, that culminated is us raiding the palace kitchen for snacks and going down to the beach to watch the sunrise.

"I can't believe how beautiful everything is," Kelsey said, as the sky began to lighten. "Kilstiffen's always been amazing, but now that it's above water it's a whole new level."

"I know what you mean," I said. "It's a shame it has to go below again."

"Why does it have to go below?" Kevin mused.

"Um, to keep the surface world from looking over and saying hey, there's a whole new country over there," I pointed out. "It's not safe out in the open like this."

"But Evonium remains above," Kevin said. "And parts of Ker Ys are always visible. Perhaps Kilstiffen doesn't need to remain below for seven years at a stretch."

"Isn't it also guarding the way below?" Aodhan asked. "Keeping nosy mortals out of the gods' land, and the monsters from sneaking above?"

"Monsters manage to find their way above regardless," Kevin replied, "but you've got a point. However, I am going to ask Grand-father about getting the place up in the sunlight more often. It would probably do the city some good."

"Agreed," I said. "Since Evonium's always above, you should talk to Scáthach, too."

"She's disappeared with Fionn," Kelsey said. "Just like how your parents ran off together as soon as they saw each other, and Rose lured Oscar off somewhere private. Face it, Kilstiffen is an island of lovers."

Kevin wrapped his arm around her shoulders and kissed the top of her head. "You're not wrong, Kels."

I leaned against Aodhan, content not only for myself, but for my family as well. We'd all made it through one ordeal after another, each more harrowing than the last, and we not only survived. We triumphed.

One person who did not triumph was Corentin. He'd been left behind at Ker Ys, and put in the same cell Dahut had imprisoned Gradlon in. As for what his ultimate fate would be, Gradlon was content to let his brother sit there and rot while he considered the proper punishment. I hoped he would remain there for a long, long time.

Gradlon also remained at Ker Ys to help rebuild everything his children and brother had damaged. It was a daunting task, but Grandfather was prepared to lend Ker Ys whatever aid was needed. When I asked what would ultimately become of the land, since Gradlon's heirs were now far off in the Northern Reaches with Ran, Grandfather revealed that that had already been worked out.

"Gradlon has decreed that if he passes on without an heir, Ker Ys will go to my own children, and then to my grandchildren," Grandfather replied. We were in the noon room again, but this time our entire family was present, along with everyone's assorted spouses and loved ones. It was a tight fit, but oh so wonderful having everyone together. "What that means, Meri, is that both you and Kevin could rule your own cities, one day."

"Oh, I don't know about that," I said. "Why not let Kevin have Kilstiffen, and Oscar can look after Ker Ys?"

"A good plan," Kevin said. "Kelsey can help me, make sure I keep myself grounded and don't get too many outlandish ideas."

Kelsey snorted. "As if anyone can calm that racing mind of yours."

"That's good for Kevin, but Oscar can barely look after himself," Scáthach said. Next to her, Fionn laughed behind his mug of ale. "Ker Ys wouldn't last a month."

"I'm sitting right here," Oscar grouched.

"It wouldn't be so bad," Mama said. "He's got Rose to keep him in line, and she's quite levelheaded."

"Again, right here," Oscar said.

"Gradlon did offer me his kingdom," Rose said. "Oscar would make a find castle steward, though."

Oscar glared at us while we laughed. "Meri, I've no doubt that you will one day do great things, be they in Kilstiffen or elsewhere," he said. "As for my sisters, they'd both best sleep with one eye open."

"And me?" Rose asked.

"You, my queen, may sleep soundly, and dream only of sweet things," he said. "And I do have a crown in my storeroom that would look wonderful with your silky brown pelt."

Kevin did speak with Grandfather about keeping the city at least partly aloft. Grandfather agreed that surfacing more often may be for the best, and agreed to consider the idea. After the city retreated as Manannán had planned, we all went home.

Three days after we returned to our old farmhouse in County Clare, Da baked a cake and we celebrated my birthday. Only my parents, Kevin and Kelsey, Aodhan, and I were present, but I preferred it that way. After we'd eaten and the rest sang to me, Aodhan and I piled into his car (that had somehow been returned to our driveway from where we'd left it in County Antrim, most likely by a benevolent sea god we all knew and loved) and he took me to the new bookstore down in Cork.

"See? Birthday bookstore trip, just like I promised," he said, as we careened down the narrow roads, scaring sheep and locals alike.

"I can't believe you remember than promise." He'd made it before we'd met Dahut and Nahel or faced Donn, back when we were still trying to define what was growing between us. "But I'm glad you did."

"As if I would forget." He squeezed my knee. "Now that our lives are somewhat back to normal, what do you want to do next?"

What, indeed. My mind swam with all the things I could tell him; we still hadn't decided if we wanted to live at the farmhouse, above the surf shop, or somewhere else entirely. There was also the looming question of marriage, in that Aodhan had asked me and I hadn't really answered him. Not to mention, I was on track to inherit a magical sea kingdom.

But today was my birthday bookstore trip, and I didn't want to deal with any of that.

"Why don't we let our next adventure find us," I suggested. "Until it does, we can enjoy every day as it comes."

"Perfect, Mer," Aodhan said. "That sounds just perfect."

While we're waiting for Meri and Aodhan's next adventure, read all about how Brian met Aoife in *A Sea of Secrets and Salvation*, available here: https://www.amazon.com/dp/B0DVKSFPP7

Turn the page for a sneak peek!

A SEA OF SECRETS AND SALVATION

Here are the first two chapters of A Sea of Secrets and Salvation. Enjoy!

Chapter One – Aoife

"This is a fine mess," I grumbled. I kicked a rock, which didn't move but hurt my foot, nonetheless. Add that ache to my wounded sword arm, strained throat, and other lingering issues, and I was a sorry excuse for a warrior. "This never would have happened to Scáthach."

I considered Scáthach. Not only was she my elder sister, she was a right terror, and spent her days leading a military academy located off the coast of Scotland. A wise woman would have reached out to her sister for aid, or at least advice, before first arguing with the king, and then plunging headlong into a situation that was larger and more complex than anyone realized. But not me. I'd run off and done things my own way, and now I was wounded and stranded on a beach at the base of the Cliffs of Moher.

Worst of all, I was stranded above.

Furious, mostly with myself, I paced the length of the beach. The two men who'd led me to my unfortunate situation were Gradlon, the monarch of Ker Ys, and a captain of my home city of Kilstiffen's guard called Seamus MacCreehy. Gradlon hadn't been foolish enough to raise his hand to me; no, he had approached me with a treaty of sorts, and while it wasn't anything that physically harmed me it was a blow nonetheless. And the fact that my father had agreed with Gradlon had hurt further still.

As for Seamus, he was committing nothing short of treason, and I said as much. I'd no sooner drawn my sword when his guards surrounded me. Mindless sycophants, all of them. Even so, those sycophants had effectively kept me from their leader, and one of them landed a lucky blow to my shoulder that rendered my sword arm all but useless. I'd had no choice but to use the magic imbued in my voice to escape the city and then flee upward through the sea, and now my throat was so raw I could barely muster a whisper.

Gods below, I had no idea how I'd get off this beach and back home.

A thrumming sound roused me from my dark thoughts. I looked toward the sea, and saw a white craft on the horizon. The idiot on the boat was back.

"Hello again," the man operating the boat called over. "Have you changed your mind about me coming ashore?"

"Don't you dare come any closer," I screeched, my voice raspier than it usually was thanks to the pain in my throat. "Set foot on this beach and I'll cut off your head!"

"Suit yourself," he said, then he threw two items onto the beach. Assuming they were weapons of a sort, I stood my ground but kept a sharp eye on the projectiles. Boat Man laughed, and I turned my scowl toward him. He was a young man, with cropped dark hair and a ghost of a beard along his jaw. He'd removed his shirt since he'd last come by to taunt me, and his well-muscled arms and chest were on full display. Boat Man was a handsome idiot, I'd give him that.

"Leave me," I croaked as I flung my arm toward the sea. The movement strained my bad shoulder, and I bit the inside of my mouth to keep from crying out. I'd learned long ago to not show any weakness, physical or otherwise, especially not in front of a *surface dweller*.

Boat Man saw me wince as I held my arm against my body, but he didn't comment on my obvious pain. Instead, he turned the boat around and left, which was all I'd wanted from him. After the craft was out of sight, I approached the missiles he'd lobbed onto the beach. They were two bottles, clear like glass but much lighter, and more pliable. I got one of them open, and found that it contained cool, clean water. I scanned the horizon, and wondered if I'd been too hasty in my treatment of the man. Perhaps he'd spoken the truth, and only wanted to help me. My gaze dropped to the shore, and the sea. It moved closer and closer to my feet as the tides came in.

Perhaps I should have accepted his aid.

Perhaps I should form a real plan, instead of feeling sorry for myself.

I drank more water, which felt like knives against my raw throat. I only needed to allow my throat time to heal, then I would sing and swim my way out of this mess. Soon enough, I would be home, and Seamus would pay for his crimes. As for Gradlon's mad plans, getting around him will take a bit more finesse. Sadly, if there was anything I lacked, it was finesse.

Chapter Two – Brian

I lay awake all night, thinking about her. The woman on the beach. The way the sunlight had glinted off her pale hair, how her eyes were a bright, clear blue—and the anger flashing in those depths. Add to her obvious beauty her odd clothing and assortment of weaponry, and the lady on the beach was quite the enigma.

I couldn't understand how she'd ended up on that beach, which was nothing more than a thin sliver of land at the base of the near-vertical cliffs. She certainly didn't swim there or climb down from above, and there were no crafts moored nearby. What's more I asked around at the piers, and no women had been reported missing. It was as if I'd wandered into a fairy tale and met a selkie or siren who'd been waylaid on her journey home... Which would have explained the ethereal singing I'd heard. Following that song was what led me right to the beach, but that woman only screeched and croaked at me. She couldn't have been the one singing such a lovely tune, but if it hadn't been her voice I heard whose was it?

Magical creatures aside, not only did she need to get off that beach, she was wounded. I recalled how she'd favored her right arm, and the rest of her looked rather beat up as well. Even though she threatened me with a beheading, what she needed was help, and I was going to get her some whether she wanted it or not.

As soon as I got out of bed. I phoned the Coast Guard and gave them her coordinates, then I went down to my boat and headed over to where I'd last seen her. High tide had been at around three in the morning, and for the life of me I couldn't remember if the beach she was on ever got fully submerged. My gut clenched, and as I steered my craft toward the cliffs, I hoped things hadn't taken a turn for the worse.

When I approached the beach and saw her stalking the length of it like a trapped panther, I breathed a sigh of relief. She was still wearing that odd kit of gold chain mail and leather armour and boots, not that she had luggage with her for a wardrobe change. In fact, aside from her clothing the only items she had were a round shield strapped to her back, a set of wide gold bracelets on her wrists, and a sword belted at her hip.

I swung the boat around and cut the engine so she could hear me. "I see you survived the night."

"Aye," she replied, but her voice was much weaker than it had been the day prior.

"I've some food and water with me, and I'd like to share it with you," I continued. "Am I allowed to come ashore, or am I still in danger of losing my head?"

She didn't speak, but waved me toward the beach. Taking that as my invitation I dropped anchor, then I launched the life raft. I'd already stocked it with food, water, a first aid kit, and a few towels. After I'd reached the shore and dragged the raft onto the beach, I offered her a bottle of water.

"It's fresh," I said, when she stared at it as if she'd never seen a plastic bottle before, as if this wasn't identical to the bottles I'd tossed out to her yesterday. I twisted off the cap, and held it out to her. "Want me to drink a bit, and prove to you it's not poisoned?"

She frowned, and shook her head. "Thank you," she rasped, then she drank. "Gods below, thank you for that."

"You're quite welcome. Would you like to sit?" I grabbed one of the towels—the old ratty ones always got demoted to boat duty, a habit I'd learned from my mum—and spread it across the rocky beach. It wouldn't be much of a cushion against the rocks, but at least it was dry. "I've some food, if you're hungry."

"Why are you helping me?" she demanded.

"Because you need help," I replied. "You're obviously stranded out here. I know I'm a stranger to you, but I mean you no harm. If you're willing to get on my boat, I'll take you to the harbor, and then you can be on your way."

"What harbor?" she asked.

"I usually dock at Liscannor, but Doolin's the closest." When her only response was to look toward the sea, I asked, "Is there another harbor you'd like to go to, instead?"

"Doolin? That's the village across from Inisheer?" she asked, naming the closest of the Aran Islands.

"Aye, that's the one."

"They'll find me in Doolin," she murmured. "I need a different place to go ashore, somewhere they won't look for me. I cannot return below before I'm ready."

"Mmm." I had no idea what she meant by that, since the only thing below us was the ocean floor. Instead of pointing that out I busied myself by sorting through the food I'd brought. Hunger and thirst had been known to drive a person mad. "I brought some energy bars. They taste awful, but if it's calories you're needing they'll do the job. I've also got some apples, and bread." I tore off a portion of bread and handed it to her. "My name is Brian, by the way. Brian Murphy."

"I'm called Aoife," she replied. "You must think I'm crazy."

"I think you've been stuck on this beach for at least a full day and night, and that's enough to drive anyone off the deep end." I jerked my chin toward the bread. "Go on. Try it."

Aoife accepted the bread and smiled, and damn it all but that smile went straight to my heart. "It's very good," she said, after she'd had a bite. "Do you live on your boat?"

"It seems that way sometimes, but no," I replied. "I have a house. It's an old farm. Hasn't had a decent crop in years, though I want to start growing again. My dream is to open a restaurant and serve locally grown produce, and seafood caught on my own boat." I paused my rambling, and wondered why I was telling her all of that. I grabbed one of the apples, and offered it to Aoife. "These apples are from my wee orchard."

Aoife took the apple from me, and scrutinized it as if I'd handed her a rare jewel. "App ell," she repeated, stretching out the syllables. "I don't think we have these where I'm from."

Where in the world were apples an oddity? "Are you from far away?"

"It's rather close, actually. How does one eat one of these?"

"I can cut it up for you," I began, then a knife appeared in her hand.

"I can handle slicing it up." She deftly sliced off two portions, and held one out to me. "Have some with me?" I took the piece from her, warily since I still had no idea where that knife came from. "Oh, it's sweet! And crunchy!"

"Have the rest," I said, when she offered me a second slice. She didn't need to be told twice, and I watched as Aoife gobbled down the rest of the apple.

"I see what you're doing, Brian Murphy," Aoife said, as she sliced the last bits of white flesh from the apple's core.

"Oh? What's that, now?"

"You've come onto my beach bearing cool water and exotic treats as your final attempt to get me on that boat of yours," she said, with a sidelong glance at me.

"This is your beach? I was not aware."

"I was here first, so that makes it mine."

"Ah. I stand corrected," I said, as Aoife's smile grew into a full grin. I'd never seen a lovelier sight in all my days. "Has my plan worked?"

"It surely has, and it's been helped along by the fact that I cannot bear to spend another moment on this rocky, soggy bit of sand." She stood, though she still favored her right side. "If your offer still stands, that is."

"Of course it does." I gathered up the few items I'd brought with me and stowed them in the raft, then I faced Aoife. "Before we push off, I need to know how many knives you have on you."

She tensed. "Why is that?"

"The raft's inflatable. A stray poke and we'll be swimming for it."

Aoife tossed back her head and laughed. "Afraid of a dip in the cold water? Fear not, Brian Murphy. Not only do I have excellent control of my blades, I'm a strong swimmer. I won't let you drown."

"Consider me reassured." With that, Aoife got onto the raft, and as I pushed off from the beach, I wondered what I was getting myself into.

Keep reading about when Aoife met Brian here: https://www.amazon.com/dp/B0DVKSFPP7

GLOSSARY OF PEOPLE, PLACES, AND PRONUNCIATIONS

Ankou (AN koo) – a creature who collects the souls of the dead and brings them to hell.

Aodhan (AY den) Sullivan – owner of Sullivan's Surf Shop, son of Lucas and Bridgette, and Meri's partner in all things.

Aoife (EE fah) Murphy – a merrow and warrior from Kilstiffen. Mother of Kevin and Meri, wife of Brian, sister of Oscar and Scáthach, and daughter of Steinar and Niamh.

Brian Murphy – a fisherman with dreams of running a restaurant. Father of Kevin and Meri, husband of Aoife.

<u>Camargue (Kah marg)</u> – water horses that live in the marshes near Ker Ys.

<u>Céilí (KAY lee)</u> – a gathering where those in attendance dance and play traditional Irish music. These gatherings may be held in a home or a public location.

<u>Cliffs of Moher</u> – sea cliffs located at the southwestern edge of the Burren region in County Clare, Ireland. They run for about fourteen kilometres. At their southern end, they rise one hundred twenty metres above the Atlantic Ocean at Hag's Head, and, eight kilometres to the north, they reach their maximum height of two hundred fourteen metres just north of O'Brien's Tower, then continue at lower heights. The closest settlements are the villages of Liscannor six kilometres to the south, and Doolin seven kilometres to the north.

<u>Corentin (kor en tin)</u> – prince of Ker Ys and younger brother of Gradlon.

<u>Dahut (DA het)</u> – princess of Ker Ys. Daughter of Gradlon, twin sister of Nahel.

<u>Donn Dhumach (don DOO mahk)</u> – sidhe prince and master of the dead.

<u>Evonium (ee VO nee um)</u> – a lost city off the western coast of Scotland.

<u>Gancanagh</u> – a male fairy known for seducing women.

<u>Gaol</u> – prison.

<u>Garda</u> – The Garda Síochána is the national police and security service of Ireland. It is more commonly referred to as the Gardaí or the Guards.

<u>Giant's Causeway</u> – a formation of tens of thousands of basalt columns on Northern Ireland's coast.

<u>Gradlon Mor</u> – the king of Ker Ys, father of Dahut and Nahel, older brother of Corentin.

Great Famine – also called the Great Hunger, was a period of mass starvation and disease in Ireland from 1845 to 1849.

Kelsey McGrath – classmate of Meri, partner to Kevin.

Ker Ys (Kerr Iss) – a mythical city on the coast of Brittany that was swallowed up by the ocean.

Kevin Murphy – half merrow and heir of Kilstiffen. He is the son of Aoife and Brian, brother of Meri, partner to Kelsey.

Kilstiffen – a lost city beneath the Cliffs of Moher which sprawls grandly over the Atlantic Ocean on the western coast of Ireland. The city once rose every seventh year, but now it remains submerged until the golden key to the gates is found.

Lucas Sullivan – father of Aodhan, Mary, and Anne. Former surfing champion from California, he was held captive by Seamus MacCreehy for eight years.

Manannán mac Lir (MAH na non mac LEER) – god of the sea, father of Niamh, grandfather of Aoife.

Meredith "Meri" Murphy – half merrow and the heiress of Kilstiffen, she commanded a stone army and defeated Seamus MacCreehy. She's the daughter of Aoife and Brian, sister of Kevin, and partner to Aodhan.

Merrow – a mermaid or merman in Irish folklore.

Milesians – the Milesians (sons of Míl) are Gaels who sailed to Ireland from Iberia. When they landed in Ireland they fought with the Tuatha Dé Danann. The two groups agreed to divide Ireland between them: the Milesians took the world above, while the Tuatha Dé Danann took the world below.

Mo chroí (moh cree) – my heart in Irish.

Nahel (NA hell) – prince of Ker Ys, son of Gradlon, twin brother of Dahut.

<u>Niamh (neev)</u> – daughter of Manannán mac Lir, wife of Steinar, mother of Aoife, Oscar, and Scáthach.

<u>Ogham (og hmm)</u> – an Early Medieval alphabet used primarily to write the early Irish language, and later the Old Irish language.

<u>Oisín (oh sheen)</u> – regarded in legend as the greatest poet of Ireland. He spent three years in the Otherworld with the sea god's daughter, but it was three hundred years in mortal time. When he returned to Ireland the centuries caught up to him, and as soon as his foot touched Irish soil he withered and died.

<u>Oscar</u> – son of Niamh and Steinar, brother of Aoife and Scáthach.

<u>Press</u> – Irish term for a cabinet or cupboard.

<u>Ran</u> – Norse sea goddess.

<u>Saint Senan and Conainne's Academy (The Saints)</u> – the school Meri and Aodhan attend.

<u>Scáthach (skah hoch)</u> – the head of the combat training academy in Evomium. Daughter of Steinar and Niamh, sister of Aoife and Oscar.

<u>Seamus MacCreehy (Shay muss Mah kree hee)</u> – a merrow and once captain in Kilstiffen's army who attempted to permanently raise the city. He was defeated by Meri.

<u>Selkie (sell key)</u> – creatures that can shapeshift between seal and human forms by removing or putting on their seal skin.

<u>Sidhe (shee)</u> – the fairy folk of Ireland, said to live in underground palaces or forts called sidhe.

<u>Steinar (STAI nar) the Immoveable</u> – king of Kilstiffen, husband of Niamh, father of Scáthach, Oscar, and Aoife.

<u>Tallulah (tah LOO lah)</u> – also known as Tourmaline, Jewel of the Sea. A stone merrow and cousin to Aoife.

<u>Tech Duinn (tek doon)</u> – literally the house of the dead, where Donn Dhumach collects the souls of the dead.

<u>Time Team</u> – long-running British archaeology programme.

<u>Tír na nÓg (teer nah nogue)</u> – In Irish mythology, Tír na nÓg or Tír na hÓige ('Land of Youth') is one of the names for the Celtic Otherworld.

<u>Tuatha Dé Danann (too AH de Dan an)</u> – literally, "the folk of the goddess Danu". They comprise the Irish pantheon of gods who dwell in the Otherworld.

Also by Jennifer Allis Provost

The Order of the Phoenix
The Phoenix and the Cat
Phoenix Rising
Dragon Descending
The Chronicles of Parthalan, a six volume epic fantasy (and one short story collection)
Heir to the Sun
The Virgin Queen
Rise of the Deva'shi
Pieces of Parthalan: Six All-New Stories From The Land of Parthalan
Golem
Elfsong
Sunfall

The Copper Legacy, a four book urban fantasy:
Copper Girl
Copper Ravens
Copper Veins
Copper Princess

A duology based in the Copper world:

Redemption

Salvation

Poison Garden, an urban fantasy filled with seers, witches, and one seriously hot detective:

Belladonna

Oleander

Bleeding Hearts

Thornapple

Wolfsbane

Mistletoe

Mandrake

Gallowglass, an urban fantasy set in Scotland and New York:

Gallowglass

Walker

Homecoming

The Shades of Elphame

Winter's Queen, an urban fantasy set in Scotland and Elphame:

Touch of Frost

Giant's Daughter

Elphame's Queen

Merrowkin, an urban fantasy set in Ireland above and below

Merrowkin

Death's Door

Manannán's Pearl

A Sea of Secrets and Salvation

Changes, a contemporary romance:

Changing Teams
Changing Scenes
Changing Fate
Changing Dates

ABOUT THE AUTHOR

Jennifer Allis Provost is a native New Englander who lives in a sprawling colonial along with her beautiful and precocious twins, a dog that thinks she's a kangaroo, a parrot, a junkyard cat, and a wonderful husband who never forgets to buy ice cream. As a child, she read anything and everything she could get her hands on, including a set of encyclopedias, but fantasy was always her favorite. She spends her days drinking vast amounts of coffee, arguing with her computer, and avoiding any and all domestic behavior.

Find Jenn on the web here: http://authorjenniferallisprovost.com/

For up to the minute sale notifications, follow her on Bookbub here: https://www.bookbub.com/profile/jennifer-allis-provost

For exclusive content, follow her on Patreon: https://www.patreon.com/jenniferallisprovost/

Friend her on Facebook: http://www.facebook.com/jennallis

Follow her on Instagram: @jenniferaprovost

Happy reading!